THE SECRET OF TWO BROTHERS

Irene Beltrán Hernández

PIÑATA BOOKS
HOUSTON, TEXAS
1995

This volume is made possible through grants from the National Endowment for the Arts (a federal agency) and the Andrew W. Mellon Foundation.

Piñata Books are full of surprises!

Piñata Books
An Imprint of Arte Público Press
University of Houston
452 Cullen Performance Hall
Houston, Texas 77204-2004

Cover illustration and design by Gladys Ramirez

Hernández, Irene Beltrán, 1945–
    The secret of two brothers / by Irene Beltrán Hernández.
        p.   cm.
    ISBN 1-55885-142-9 (paper)
    I. Title.
    PS3558.E6873S43   1995
    813'.54—dc20   95-9844
                                            CIP

♾ The paper used in this publication meets the requirements of the American National Standard for Permanence of Paper for Printed Library Materials Z39.48-1984.

1 2 3 4 5 6 7 8 9 0   13 12 11 10 9 8 7 6 5 4

In memory of the late Joe Columbus Miller (July 10, 1939–December 10, 1991) of the Seminole Nation of Oklahoma and member of the Jaycee-Zaragoza Recreation Center staff. He dedicated his life to the happiness and well-being of thousands of young people of West Dallas and asked nothing more from them than a happy smile. Great Spirits bless him.

THE SECRET OF TWO BROTHERS

CHAPTER ONE

Beaver stood straight, suddenly frightened of the sounds that echoed throughout the cell block. He tightly shut his eyes. Many times late at night the sounds would disturb his sleep, but tonight they were unusually loud and vigorous. Perhaps there were two or more guards coming. "Bulls" the prisoners called them. He knew for a fact that their faces would be drawn into a hard frown, harder than the concrete floor beneath his cot. Beaver could never stop the echo of their boots which beat savagely upon the gray tiles as they moved toward his cell. The skin covering his neck pricked with roused goose pimples. He jumped down from his cot, then quickly moved to the bars that secured the entrance of his cell and stared down the catwalk, but still he could not see them.

Beaver nervously glanced at the barred window of his sparse cell. Outside, the night sky was filled with lightning streaks. Sheets of rain slapped against the outside concrete walls. Thunder caused bolts of light to flash across his chest as he looked helplessly toward the heavens. It was his night to die, he thought. Beads of perspiration oozed on his forehead as paced back and forth like a caged cougar. His skittish pacing vibrated throughout the cell row, drowning out the sounds of the guards as they moved toward him. What have I done now, he wondered? He gripped the iron bars tightly. Had he gotten so confident of himself and of his ability to get out of the many tight situations that occurred in prison? Had the guards finally realized that he had bought his way out of many skirmishes by giving extra helpings of food to other prisoners? He shook his head sadly. He never believed in forgiveness of sins. And, he had committed many sins. But in his own mind he saw forgiveness as a man-made word...a word used much too often in this stinking prison. All prisoners screamed forgiveness at one time or another, especially if they were being beaten by the other prisoners. Beaver didn't care at all about forgiveness! To him it was a wobbly word... unconcrete like jello. He had learned early in life not to forgive or forget.

He remembered a time long ago when he had hung around street corners with an outstretched hand begging for money. "Hustle" was the word he had been trained to use, not forgiveness. No one ever spoke of forgiveness to him on the outside world, not even his departed mother.

"Hustle, Francisco!" his father had always said. "Hustle for the dough, for the money. Hustle for what you want because nobody else is gonna do it for you." His father had laughed crazily like he always did when he'd had too many beers. Then he'd coldly added, "And, Francisco, women are the easiest to hustle!" It had not mattered one bit that his mother was in the room and had heard his father's comment. It had not mattered that his father had hurt his mother's feelings. It was as if his father had stabbed her and left her lying on the floor to bleed to death. Beaver had realized that his mother's heart had broken and that she had held nothing but the best intentions.

A tear fell from Beaver's eye. He quickly wiped it away. In a low, despairing voice, he cursed his father. All the man cared about was hustling for dope and chasing other women. Beaver's grandmother had told him years ago that his father was cruel because of the beatings his own father inflicted upon him. When Beaver had asked her why she did not stop the punishment and beatings, she had commented that she had tried many times, but it seemed to be an inbred conflict between a father and his first son.

"And many times, Beaver, your father deserved his beatings. Often he talked back to his father in ugly words. That was one of his greatest faults. Your father could not keep his mouth shut."

In some ways, Beaver considered himself no better than his father. He'd hustled on street corners for food, for a dime, for a quarter, for money to purchase milk and bread for his little brother, Cande, and himself. He'd been forced to be a beggar and to do whatever he needed to survive. Cande had depended on him.

Beaver gripped the bars of his cell door and remembered Cande as a four-year-old sitting under a tree, not far from the corner where Beaver hustled people coming out of the Alamo, the only large grocery store in the area. Occasionally, Beaver would glance back at Cande and see the child stare back at him with his big, sad, almond-shaped black eyes. Even little Cande had to depend on handouts until the first of each month when the welfare checks normally arrived.

Beaver had promised that he would never let Cande hustle. He would die before something like that happened to his little brother. And yet, at this moment, sitting here in prison waiting to find out what the Bulls wanted, Beaver felt dead, as dead as a bloated fish floating across the river, riding the waves because it no longer had the strength nor the will to submerge to the bottom of the murky river.

Tears burned his eyes. Ashamed, he commanded them to stop! *Vatos* like me don't cry, he thought. It's not macho to cry.

But deep inside his heart, he was afraid. Beaver shivered. His sweat felt cold upon his forehead. In this stinking prison Beaver had always been afraid of the other guys, afraid of the gangs, the drugs and the dirty needles.

Beaver's life three years earlier had been filled with feeding Cande, with bright sunny colors in a world that contrasted with the depressing gray hues of the prison. And, now...his tears could not stop. The fears like the ones which presently gripped him never diminished, as they had in the days of his adolescence. As he matured, his fears increased daily. The menacing gangs that plagued the ranks of prison life particularly scared him.

The gangs wielded the sword that gave life or death. Such a death would never be questioned by the prison authorities. Such a death certificate would indicate simply that the prisoner had died of infection or complications from surgery that suddenly went wrong.

In prison the norms were as radical as the politics of the outside world. That first year in prison, Beaver's spirit had shriveled in agony. He'd been beaten constantly by the older inmates, but he had stood his ground. He was trapped in a living hell, but determined to survive as he had in the barrio, for he had to survive for Cande.

And now, the guard's footsteps echoed as they hurried down the dim corridor rattling their keys in their hands as though they too were nervous. Maybe they weren't coming for him...maybe they'd stop at some other cell. Maybe this situation was just a very bad dream. Yes, he laughed wildly, like in the dream that kept waking him each morning before dawn. The dream filled with ugly demons that crept up from under his cot to grab and eat away at his vulnerable skin.

Beaver took a deep breath to calm himself, then quickly wiped his forehead with his shaky hand. He leaned against the bars for support because at this moment his energy seemed to evaporate into nothing.

"Francisco?" His neighboring cellmate Juan quietly called. "What's happening, Francisco?"

"It's me they're coming for. I can feel it!" Beaver replied in a quiet whisper.

"What'd you do?" Juan asked.

"Hey, what do I have to do? I was just born... that's all!"

"Be cool, Beaver," Juan advised. "Don't give them reason to beat you." Juan stuck his hand outside the bars of his cell and gave the two-finger victory sign.

Beaver was worried. He had been worried since the previous night when one of the older trustees had approached him and pulled him aside, promising information in exchange for an unopened pack of cigarettes. At lunch the following day, Beaver had traded an extra slice of apple pie for a pack of cigarettes. Late that same night, he had met the old trustee.

The old trustee had a fearful gleam in his eyes as he said, "The parole board gets your case tomorrow evening. You're up for parole. I saw your records." He nodded knowingly, smiled, then nervously glanced toward the entrance to the showers. "Good luck!" he added as he slipped through the shower-stall door.

Beaver stood rooted to the cold tiles of the shower floor. He was flabbergasted! He hadn't heard a word about parole from Sánchez, his attorney. Had time in prison been so laden with daily hardships that he'd lost track of the passing days? He had already lost three years of his life to this hellhole. The days and nights had blended into one another, creating a downslide of lost, irretrievable time. At that moment he felt an urgent need to speak with Sánchez, but getting to a phone at that time was impossible.

Beaver had quickly showered and hurried back to his cell. He hadn't been looking for trouble at that time of night. He had laid still upon his mattress, listening to the pounding of his heart. "Go to sleep, Francisco Torres," he had said to himself with no avail.

"Lady," he had prayed to the tattooed Virgin de Guadalupe he carried upon his back. "Lady, you've been with me for a long time. You alone understand where I'm coming from, no?" He had spoken to her softly, as if she had been his real mother. "You know I didn't hurt nobody. Yeah," he whispered, "you and I know that I didn't do anything wrong. I'm not a bad person. I'm really not, you know that.

"Lady, I've got to survive this prison. Get me out of this black pit of demons. How are you gonna help me out of this mess?" he asked as he nervously rubbed the stubble on his chin. "I'm too young to be trapped. I've just turned twenty-one and everything I did, I did for Cande. You know that." He rose and quietly paced back and forth, whispering to the beautiful lady etched in black ink upon his muscular back. He remembered his *abuelita* telling him about the Virgin's appearance on Mount Tepeyac in Mexico to an Indian named Juan Diego.

Beaver had been fascinated by the story because Juan Diego was a short guy much like himself who had climbed to the top of Mount Tepeyac without shoes. Yes, this Juan Diego was a strong Indian and Beaver admired him. He remembered how his *abuelita's* ebony eyes had glowed as if the stars themselves reflected in them whenever she spoke of this special Lady. The Virgin, she had said, had an iridescent-like shine in her eyes. The same light illuminated the stones and cactus around her, making them gleam like brilliant diamonds. "Someday, Beaver," his *abuelita* had said, "I'll take you to see the very cloak that Juan Diego wore. It still hangs in the cathedral in Mexico City. I got to see it when I was a small girl."

Beaver stopped pacing and leaned against his cot. Thinking of his *abuelita*, he had calmed down. He smiled sadly because his abuelita never got to take him on that pilgrimage to Mexico City, but he had made a promise that if he ever got out of prison he would take a trip to see the cloak that Juan Diego wore.

The cloak had a picture of the Virgin de Guadalupe on it and had not deteriorated after so many centuries. He promised that he would take roses of all colors for the Virgin as well.

The night before, Beaver had dreamed of Margie, his first girlfriend. He had been in the eighth grade when he went steady with her. A long-legged girl, she had been a born tease and he knew that, but it hadn't bothered him as long as she smiled at him. Her long black hair had been thick and wavy and had forever gotten in his way. But he loved it, especially when they were walking home from school and a strong wind spread the ebony strands in a thousand different directions. Her skin had been deeply tanned because she loved being outdoors. Her black eyes had flashed with such sparkle. In his dream, she had been going round and round on the merry-go-round, urging him to catch her. "See! You'll never catch up with me!" she had screamed.

Upon Beaver's arrival in prison, he had been immediately put to work in the prison kitchen. At first, he hated the tasks he had to do in that steel-covered room, but soon his assignments there turned out to be his salvation. He progressed rapidly from dishboy to junior pastry chef. He was taught by the senior pastry chef, an older man named Dennis who eventually started sharing trade secrets with him. From that moment on, cooking had fascinated Beaver.

"Put love into your pies and cakes. That means create them as if you were making a dessert to please the Lord," Dennis had told him. "It's like an artist in love with a particular color...like fuchsia. And this artist puts fuchsia into all his paintings. It's his trademark, see?"

Beaver nodded to the balding Dennis that he understood and quickly took to making delicious fillings, although mastering the large amounts of dough for pie crusts was tricky. But with time, Beaver got the hang of it. The end product was a joy for him to behold, and soon he was turning out ten dozen pies per day while Dennis turned out dozens of cakes.

Today, Beaver's meringue toppings were weak and his crusts hard and tasteless. Beaver's mind was not on cooking. He wanted to hear from Sánchez, who had not bothered to return his frantic calls. His temper had flared as he constantly looked at the clock and the phone-message board. As he cleaned up the kitchen after the last supper shift, he asked one of the guys if he knew when the parole board met. The guy thought it was on Thursday night, twice a year or so, but he wasn't sure.

"Does your attorney have to be present?" Beaver quizzed him.

He shook his head. "Don't think so," he replied as he bent over a pan to scrub it in soapy water. "It'll be a long time before I have to worry about a parole board, kid." He laughed crazily.

Beaver stepped away from him and backed into Dennis.

"Beaver, don't go making trouble for yourself. No parole board is worth it. You've finished your work here. Go to your cell. Take a rest."

"Sure, Dennis," Beaver answered quickly. "I was just asking, that's all."

Dennis stood looking grimly down at Beaver. "My term is twenty years and that's a long time for any man. You're young and you're not carrying twenty years on your back. You've still got a little time to serve in this prison, and tomorrow is just another hard day ahead. So, forget the parole board and get some shuteye. See you at five in the morning."

Beaver quickly left the area and headed to the recreation room to try to watch television, but he was too restless to do that. He went to his cell where he climbed into his bunk and tried reading. After a while, he threw his book to the floor. Then he heard the call for lights out and listened to the guys in his neighboring cells shout at one another as they settled in for the night. Beaver wrapped himself deeper into his blanket and tried to close his eyes, but it was impossible to rest. He turned over and lay on his stomach and finally dozed off.

Echoes from the pounding of the guards' boots woke him from his sluggish sleep. Beaver jerked his head up. The guards were coming. He glanced out his cell window trying to guess what time it was... perhaps eleven, he guessed. He listened to the pounding of the boots on the tile floor.

Juan's voice broke the silence. "Keep your mouth shut!" he reminded Beaver. "No matter what, understand?"

Suddenly the guards stood at the bars. There were two of them with flashlights. Two bulls, two guns. One guard was old, bald, and tired-looking. The other was young, eager to kick ass at the slightest provocation.

"Francisco Torres? Alias Beaver Torres?" the younger guard asked in an excited voice.

Beaver faced them, taking in their starched sand-colored uniforms. "That's me, Boss!" he answered, forcing his voice to remain steady and controlled.

"Come with us." The young guard unlocked the cell door.

"Yes, Boss!" Beaver answered as he ran his hand through his hair and nervously glanced at the older guard who looked at him with disinterest. The situation was not good. Beaver's only hope was Carl, the older guard. He carried more clout than the young bull who now stood there smirking before him. Carl would not allow beatings.

Beaver knew that from the lips of terrified prisoners whom the bulls called upon at other times. As far as Beaver knew, he was safe with Carl, who played by the rule book.

The young guard unlocked the cell door then stepped aside so Beaver could exit. Beaver faced them, took a deep breath, filled out his chest, and held his head high. This is it, he thought regretfully. He didn't like the pain they'd probably inflict upon him. He moved out of the cell and positioned himself directly behind the slightly stooped older man who appeared to be in his late fifties. The younger guard was so close to Beaver's back that he felt the man's hot steamy breath on his neck. Beaver instantly saw the rifles they carried. His muscles tightened when he realized that this situation was more serious than he realized. He glanced back, making sure that he kept at least one step ahead of them. As the trio progressed through the dimly lit catwalk, they were seen by only a few frightened prisoners who quickly lifted their heads and stared inquisitively as the procession passed their cells.

Beaver entered a brightly lit room where he was told to sit on one of two chairs in the room. The younger guard left the room as Beaver seated himself facing the door. The room was vacant except for the chair on which he was sitting and a wooden table upon which lay a clean ashtray. Beaver quickly noted there was not another exit.

Carl stood beside a phone which hung on the wall. He pulled out a package of cigarettes and lit one. He inhaled deeply, took a drag, and looked over at Beaver. Then he asked, "Want one?" He kindly held out the cigarettes to Beaver.

"Yes, Boss," Beaver answered, wanting a smoke badly but refusing to move toward Carl to take it. At first, he'd been unschooled in prison-guard relationships and had reached out to take a cigarette. His hand had been instantly crushed by a wooden club that the guard whipped out in an attempt to crush as many fingers as possible. Three years later, he was smart enough to know to wait until the cigarette was out of the package and actually handed to him.

"It's okay, Torres. I'm not that young guard. He thinks he's a mercenary and those kind of people think they control the world." He moved toward Beaver and handed him a cigarette. "I know you're anxious, but this might take longer than usual. There's women on this year's parole board." Beaver noted the bitter flash in the old guard's eyes as he talked of women, but he did not interrupt him. "Women tend to get emotional over a lot of simple things. You know how women get, don't you?"

"Yeah, Boss...I know about women." Beaver took a quick puff of the cigarette and frowned. He wasn't one for smoking, but he was extremely nervous.

Carl laughed out loud like a cowboy who'd outridden a wild bronco. "Good for you, son!" He took another drag on his cigarette, then added, "I've seen lots of prisoners, but I knew there was something different about you once I noticed that tattoo on your back. Not too many religious tattoos in this place, and it made you stand out from the others. Lots of naked women tattoos around here, but never a religious saint."

Beaver stared at him for a second, surprised that Carl had noticed him at all, much less noted his tattoo. "You're talking about my Lady, Carl. She's called the Virgin de Guadalupe. She is a great Lady. I looked up the real story about her after the tattoo was inked on my back." Beaver could not explain it, but he could feel the stiffness of his shoulders easing. "When they did the tattoo, I was drunk and had just turned sixteen." He added remorsely, "It was a shame I was drunk, but now that I know all about the virgin, I'm glad I did it."

"Never heard of her," Carl replied. "Did it hurt when they put her on?"

"If it did, I don't remember feeling much pain. Scared the shit out of me the next day, though."

Carl laughed robustly. "Bet it did!"

"Carl, this Lady is special. Your people have George Washington as a hero. Us Mexicans got this Lady of Guadalupe who we look up to. She's centuries old. She appeared in Mexico in 1531 to take up the cause of all the poor Indians who were being harassed by the rich lords of the land. This Lady, she didn't get her feet dirty by walking on the ground. Her feet never touch the ground. Juan Diego—he's the Indian she appeared to first—said she moved around on a puffy white cloud. Her mark is the rose; all colors of roses encircle her as she floats about doing her business. And, they say that if she hears your prayers, there's the smell of roses in the air, even if there aren't any roses to be seen. That's how you know she'd been listening to you."

Carl threw back his head and laughed. "This sounds like a fairy tale to me, Torres."

Beaver turned red and insisted, "No, this is true! Next time I go to the prison library, I'm gonna check out the book so you can read it yourself."

"You shouldn't believe everything you read, kid," Carl stated flatly.

Beaver suddenly felt like a fool, so he refused to say more, but Carl continued. "This probation board means serious business."

Beaver remained silent a long time before he asked, "What's happening here?"

Carl shifted nervously in his chair as if to make himself more comfortable. For an instant, Beaver thought he'd noticed Carl's gray eyes flicker. "I see. The word never got to you," he added. "Well, you're due parole. The board studies a list of names and cases and then determines who goes on parole and who doesn't this time around." He took a puff of his cigarette. "You see, those people on that board do a lot of bickering about who does or doesn't. But, it never fails as the clock nears midnight, they get tired and make decisions pretty fast. I guarantee you that by eleven-thirty tonight, they'll send a message down either to take you forward or take you back to your cell. Until they make that decision, you and I stay right here in this room."

Beaver leaned back into the chair and pressed his back into the hollow of the rough wood. He looked up at the clock. It was near eleven now.

They waited, and soon Carl was pacing back and forth, glancing nervously at the clock on the wall. "Seems to be taking longer than usual," he muttered between puffs.

"Is that good or bad?" Beaver asked in a weary voice.

"Mostly bad," Carl stated flatly as he glanced sadly at Beaver.

Beaver could see pity in his eyes, so he sat forward and placed his elbows on his knees, bracing his chin with his hands. He refused to look up at Carl, whose pity he could not tolerate. His own self-pity was stabbing him in the heart, and his eyes were burning once again. He closed them and talked silently to his Lady. Beaver begged her to realize that Cande needed him to take care of him.

Much later, Beaver realized that Carl was no longer pacing and that the silence in the room was overpowering. He raised his head and looked up. Carl sat in the chair, propped back against the wall. His eyes were closed. He was sleeping. Beaver saw the blue bags under his eyes, noticed his steady breathing, and then saw the handle of his revolver. He wanted to take the revolver from the old man and force his way out of prison, maybe even hold the old guard hostage. He glanced toward the door and strained hard to hear any sounds on the other side, but he heard nothing. Would he be able to pull out the revolver without scuffling with Carl?

If he succeeded, Carl would be fired. Beaver knew Carl was up for retirement soon, or so rumor had stated. This was of no concern to him, he reasoned. It was Carl's problem and he'd have to deal with it. All Beaver had to do was grab the gun and force Carl to lead him out of the prison into a truck or something. Then he'd be free!

Beaver rose on legs that trembled like an earth-shaking volcano. He hesitated a moment, deliberating on whether to follow through with his plans. He took a deep breath, then stepped toward Carl. It should be fairly easy, he convinced himself. Just do it! He stood directly before Carl, who slept like an exhausted baby. Beaver found himself wondering how old Carl really was. With those gringos it was difficult to really tell. Suddenly, the image of another old man appeared in his mind. Beaver saw his grandfather slumped over, asleep in his wheelchair...sleeping just as Carl was now doing, muttering in his sleep. Beaver's glance fell on Carl's outstretched legs. They were sturdy...unlike his *abuelito's* amputated legs. He waited, trying to collect his courage and lunge for the gun. Do it, Beaver! It was his *abuelito's* voice that he heard firmly shout, "No, Beaver! Don't do this! Honor me and don't do this! Think of Cande!"

Beaver reached out and gently nudged Carl's knee to wake him. "Carl," he whispered. "Wake up!" He glanced anxiously toward the door, expecting it to pop open any minute.

Carl bolted forward. Beaver moved out of his way...alarmed that Carl might shoot him.

"What the hell!" Carl shouted angrily.

"Hey, Boss!" Beaver pleaded with his arms held high in the air while Carl's hand reached doubly fast for his revolver. "You fell asleep. I didn't want you to get into trouble, so I tapped your knee."

Once he realized that his revolver was secure, Carl quickly rose and anxiously rubbed his eyes. "I guess I'm getting old," he added. A slight redness tinged his frightened face. He walked over to the door and glanced out the small cube-like window, then ambled back to where Beaver sat stiffly in the chair. "Why didn't you try to escape?" he asked as he pulled the chair directly in front of Beaver and sat down. "Other prisoners would have."

Beaver stared hard at Carl and then decided to be frank with him. "I thought about taking your gun, but I know you're fair with us prisoners. Other guys have told me about things you've done for them." Beaver hesitated before he continued. "But the real truth is that...I had...something strange happen. Just as I was about to go for your gun, I heard my grandfather's voice telling me not to try anything. That I should honor him."

Carl stared at Beaver intensely as Beaver continued. "My grandfather's been dead since I was seven-years old. I swear to you. I heard his voice... it was like an order for me not to do anything to you."

Carl merely nodded and continued to study Beaver. "For what it's worth, I believe you." He remained silent as if brooding over the matter, but then he added, "You know, Torres, I owe you for this. You could have killed me on the spot. You could have held me hostage, but you chose not to harm me for whatever reason." He held out his hand to Beaver, who shook it firmly. His grasp was tight and reassuring. He continued, "If there is anything I can ever do to help you...just call on me."

Carl took a card from his billfold and handed it to Beaver who read it and glanced up at the old guard. "You're a bookkeeper, too?"

Carl smiled. "In small towns, moonlighting is the only way to make a living. I've been up late the last couple of days finalizing accounts for a couple of clients of mine. I lost some sleep and overtaxed my mind, and here I go and fall asleep in front of a prisoner. But I'm glad it was you and not somebody like Stretch Davis."

Beaver agreed. "The Stretch would have killed you." Beaver put Carl's card in his pocket just as the door opened and another guard appeared. Carl hurriedly rose, grabbed his hat, and went to speak with him behind closed doors.

Beaver paced the floor, glancing now and then at the door through which Carl had departed. Was Carl going to squeal about the incident that just occurred? Beaver hoped not. It would cause him a lot more trouble than he needed at the moment. Anxiety consumed his nerves. He wanted the whole ordeal of his parole to end. Now, as little as he knew about Carl, he had added more doubt to the issue. The clock on the wall seemed motionless, useless to him, as it ticked steadily to the rhythm of his heart.

Finally Carl returned holding up a folder stuffed with legal-sized paper. He threw the folder down on the table, looking as if he didn't know whether to laugh or cry, but at long last his very serious look vanished and was replaced by a good-hearted grin. "You've been granted parole, Torres!"

"Are you sure?" Beaver asked in a soft, distant voice as he flopped down into the chair and hastily rubbed his eyes. "I can't believe it!"

Carl sat opposite him and opened the folder. "It's official! You've got some papers to sign, a few rules and regulations to go over. Here's the name and address of a probation officer whom you are to contact within three days after you leave prison. You'll be issued some clothes, shoes, and the things you entered prison with. Then, you're on you own." Carl hesitated, suddenly surprised at his own burst of zeal, and immediately noticed Beaver's quiet mood. Carl stopped shuffling papers and glanced at him. "I told you, son...you didn't belong in this place. I have to say that you've done one hell of a job surviving for these last three years. I know what you had to contend with that first year you were brought here."

Beaver shuddered as if Carl had suddenly slapped him. Memories too awful to remember re-emerged. Beaver had hated those nights. He hastily reached up to wipe his eyes, hoping to erase the torrid pictures from his mind. The insolent voices of the older prisoners hung in his ears, voices of older men who'd repeatedly abused him and beat him if he did not submit to their wills. Beaver raised his head proudly, for he had never submitted to their demands, not peacefully anyway. He had learned the trick. His way to survive was by driving away death and by merely slipping away into a semi-conscious state. Most often he'd wake up in the prison hospital feeling bruised, broken and empty, as if he'd awakened from the dead.

Carl reached across the table and encouragingly patted Beaver's shoulder. "Forget all that's happened. Block everything from your mind and start new. I wish you the best of luck."

Beaver received his handshake and tried to smile. "Thanks, Carl. I'll do better outside. I never want to come back to this place."

Carl nodded that he understood. "And I don't want to see you back here again."

Beaver saw that Carl's eyes were red-rimmed. Beaver found himself unable to speak.

Carl quickly added, "Let's go see Mr. Perkins, the man that signs everyone out of here. Then, you can make a phone call to have someone pick you up."

Beaver shook his head. "There isn't anyone that can pick me up. Dallas is a long way from Huntsville."

Carl glanced up, surprised. "Well, tell you what... I'm off duty in half an hour. I'll drive you to the bus station."

"Great!" Beaver exclaimed, but his face quickly fell as disappointment set in. "I don't know what's happening back home... or even if there is a home. I haven't heard from anyone in two years."

Carl silently studied Beaver, sensing the boy's loss at what to do. "I see," he responded. "Your family forgot you."

Beaver saw Carl's eyes reflect that dreadful pity and looked away toward the door. "If there is a family left," Beaver muttered.

"I know how you feel, Beaver. I've been divorced twice, so I know how it is to lose your family. Life is tough." Carl spoke in a raspy whisper and Beaver found himself leaning toward him to hear better. "But, you have a chance for a new start. Do yourself a favor, Beaver...take a vacation away from the old place. Start over in a new town. Do good things. Deal with life day to day. God's everywhere, Beaver. Talk to him."

Beaver rose hastily and went toward the small window. "I believed in God...once. He let me down a long time ago."

Carl sadly shook his head from side to side. "There's always your Lady, Beaver," he suggested softly. Then in an official-sounding voice he ordered, "Let's get on with what I have to do here, and then I'll take you to see Mr. Perkins."

Beaver went back to the table and watched Carl as he opened the folder and sat reading the documents out loud. Beaver felt himself relaxing as he stared at Carl's pale eyes. Carl concentrated on the words before him.

After the paperwork was read to Beaver, Carl rose and motioned for Beaver to follow him to see Mr. Perkins. They walked like solitary figures down a shadowy marchway toward the main office. Carl walked in front of Beaver as if the young man was no longer a threat and immediately stopped at some double doors. He knocked briskly on them and was soon allowed to enter. They entered a room where Beaver was issued new street clothes. He was given his old wallet and his watch, the one he'd had on when he was picked up.

A guard hastily pushed a paper to Beaver. "Sign here," he ordered in a voice that sounded irritated.

Beaver signed without comment, intentionally scribbling his name across the entire page. He smiled brazenly at the guard, who simply scowled at him.

"Change your clothes over there!" Mr. Perkins pointed to a small closet-like space.

Beaver took his bundle of clothes and moved over to the space indicated. He quickly changed, then glanced into the small mirror and hurriedly ran a comb through his hair. Carl waited patiently outside, pacing back and forth, causing Beaver to become anxious to leave the prison. Once again, the sound of pounding boots disturbed him. Would there be another obstacle to prevent him from tasting freedom? He hoped not. When Beaver joined Carl, the old man motioned for him to follow. Beaver noticed that Carl no longer had his revolver strapped to his hip.

He walked by Carl's side down the hallway and out the main entrance of the prison. The air smelled of fragrant pine trees. Beaver hesitated slightly and deeply inhaled, then he glanced back at the prison.

He shook his head sadly as he followed Carl to his truck.

It was almost five in the morning when Carl pulled his truck up to the bus station. He turned off the motor and glanced at Beaver. "This is it, son. Be careful."

Beaver choked. The tightness in his throat stung him. After all the time he had spent in prison, he had found a kind person, someone who was not out to cheat him or beat him. And how ironic that they should meet as he was on his way to freedom. Carl had given him a sense of hope, facilitating his exit from prison life to civilian life. And for that small ray of kindness, like the gold hue of a rainbow, Beaver was eternally thankful.

"Thanks again, Carl," Beaver managed to say.

"Now, son, if there's anything I can do for you...just call me. You have my card...you hear me?"

Beaver nodded. "I hear you, Carl." He opened the door of the truck and got out. After he let the door shut, he hurried to the entrance of the bus station, hesitating to listen to the sound of the pickup as it moved. He turned to see the pickup as it disappeared into the darkness of the empty street.

CHAPTER TWO

In the early morning hours, the bus station appeared as gray and gloomy as Beaver's former prison cell. A homeless person with newspapers carelessly thrown over his face slept on a wooden bench. With the exception of the homeless man and Beaver, who paced aimlessly, the place was deserted. The sleepy clerk in the ticket window announced that at five-thirty a.m. a bus would depart for Dallas. Beaver bought his ticket and nervously glanced about. He studied display posters, read discarded newspapers, and drank plenty of coffee. He was tired, but his thoughts would not let him sleep. His mind was filled with analyzing the true meaning of freedom, and at that moment being free was the only thing that mattered in his upturned life. Beaver knew he had to find Cande. They were going to be a family no matter what, he decided.

Beaver glanced toward the phone booth. He had no one to call to tell about his freedom and he felt lonelier that ever, as if he were the only person in the world without a family. He missed his old house, the smell of his room, and the slightly disorganized clutter of jeans, T-shirts and brightly colored bandanas. He thought of the old light bulb and socket that hung from a long electrical line from the ceiling of his room, and how it gently swayed back and forth. How it had soothed him to sleep on many a restless night.

Beaver sat down on a hard wooden bench, leaned back and glanced upward toward the ceiling, fighting the overwhelming feeling of drowning in loneliness. He could cry here and no one would see him. No one would point a finger at him and tell him he was not macho. Macho guys don't cry, he remembered. Hadn't that been drilled into his head a million times during his youth in the barrio? Now he wanted to cry on his mother's shoulder, but she was dead. He fought the urge as he stared at the clock, letting the minutes tick by. Remembering that the Lady of Guadalupe was with him, he smiled. She, at least, would never leave him...not even in death. He made a silent wish for his mother. He wanted her reincarnated into the most beautiful butterfly, and he began to imagine her flying with brightly colored wings from rose to rose with not a care or worry in the world. With that thought, Beaver fell into a light sleep.

The sounds of other voices unexpectedly awoke him. People were entering the bus station and dropping their quarters into the coffee machine. Glancing at the clock that hung high on the wall, he realized he had slept more than an hour and it would be only minutes before he started his journey northward to Dallas and to a new life.

Beaver sat up straight, then glanced at the different people around him. He wondered if any of them could tell that he was an ex-con. No one seemed to take special interest in him. He smiled to himself. He had learned long ago that no one gave a damn about him. It was as if he were a ghost, a phantom that could slip through crowds of people untouched. But he knew he existed and that he was going to live, because Cande needed him. He had survived three tough years in prison and now was vowing to find Cande and protect him for the rest of his life. He worried about what Cande had gotten himself into since their mother had passed away. He knew that Cande, now fourteen, wouldn't be the same kid he'd left three years ago. But neither was he the same guy that had left to serve time in prison three years ago.

The bus moved rapidly northward as the dawn of the new day crested over the sloping hills that bordered the highway. As Beaver tried to think clearly about his life, several unpleasant scenes found their way into his memories. His life would have been better if he'd been born into a different family, he thought. Perhaps the outcome would have been different if he'd had a better father instead of a loser he called father. He wished his mother had been more stable rather than tense and worry-ridden. Beaver would have liked to have grown up in a nice neighborhood like the ones the bus was passing through now, neighborhoods that had neatly-cut green lawns and no littered trash stacked in dark corners.

In the barrio, Beaver was one of hundreds of dirty, troublesome kids. In prison, Beaver was called "Francisco," the shy guy who completed his G.E.D., the short muscular fella who was counted among the best cooks in the prison kitchen, the soft spoken guy who could turn the worst foul-mouthed creature into a humble man by placing before him a bowl of delicious steaming pinto beans seasoned with salt pork and a thick slice of jalapeno corn bread. Those tactics had never failed to get him privileges.

The thought of food made Beaver realize how famished he'd become. In prison at this early hour of the morning, he'd be sampling blueberry muffins with margarine; then he'd be wiping his hands across his fresh, white apron. He realized that food would be a problem on the outside. In prison you got three meals a day. Out in the real world people starved. Beaver hadn't been hungry since he'd entered prison, and hunger was not a feeling he'd ignore nor forget. Now, without a job or money, he would be standing in the food-stamp line at the welfare office and stretching his food so that it would last him until the end of the month. And, if he couldn't find Cande, he might have to live in the homeless shelter for a while. In prison, he'd heard many guys say that they'd broken probation just to get back into prison to have access to three meals per day and a roof over their heads.

Beaver lifted his legs onto the vacant seat next to him. As he looked out at the small farms that dotted the landscape, a new thought occurred to him. He must meet his probation officer in Dallas. He wasn't too thrilled about meeting this person and he didn't know much about probation officers except that they were constantly on one's tail about something. Having to report to a probation officer was like having one wrist handcuffed to the prison system and the other hand outstretched, ready to be slapped if it touched anything sinful. Would he ever be free to relax without worrying about covering his back?

Beaver pulled out the card that the prison official had given him. It looked official. The State of Texas seal was stamped securely on it. The name printed on the card was simply C. Rodríguez. On the back of the card, the official had hastily written the date. In three days, Beaver was to meet this probation officer at an address located in downtown Dallas. One more thing for him to worry about.

Hours later the bus arrive in Dallas. He left the station and stood on a street corner for a while, watching people pass him. Businessmen in pin-striped suits never looked his way; yet they made him feel shabby. Secretaries in varied hairdos and nylon-covered legs walked past him. At the entrance to the bus station, he saw a sharply dressed dope dealer staging his "cool" approach deals. With him was a fine-looking Afro-American hooker wearing black leather shorts, boots, and a mink jacket.

Color exploded in his mind...colors that he had missed terribly, colors that welcomed him home.

He boarded the #39 Ledbetter bus and walked toward the rear. The policeman standing guard at the back of the bus was a new item, and Beaver avoided him by sitting in the middle section of the bus.

Things had changed in Dallas while he'd been gone. The two-lane street that had crossed through West Dallas was now a six-lane thoroughfare. He was impressed with the progress of the city. Fast-food restaurants were on corners. Garza still had his bakery in the same spot, and the Sundown Market still monopolized the grocery business, even though the bus had passed several new Mexican specialty-food stores. The traffic was heavy, and as they rode several miles into the barrio, passengers kept getting on and off the bus. These people he instantly recognized as the very poor of West Dallas.

When the bus passed the projects, Beaver stared unbelievingly. Hundreds of apartments were boarded up, deserted and dilapidated. The roofs had peeled as the hot summer sun scorched them, causing them to curl. The place was worse than the prison he had just left. He exited the bus and stared at the street sign on the corner which read "Tumalo Trail," the old street where he used to live. When he was younger, Beaver thought that Native Americans lived in the area because of the names given to the various streets: Ottaway, Iroquois, Tallyho and

Pueblo. Now, only Hispanics lived in this barrio, even though the streets still bore the old names. Joe Columbus, who ran the recreation center in the neighborhood, was the only Native American Beaver knew in the area.

As he walked homeward, meeting no one he recognized, it suddenly dawned on him that the streets had been paved after many years. He remembered his mother screaming at him to wipe the mud off his shoes. Poor Mama. When she'd died, the prison chaplain had visited Beaver in his cell. He had stayed with him for a long while, explaining that his mother's death was unexpected. Beaver had not asked too many questions. He had wanted to leave her alone in death and in peace. He had just hoped that his mother had laid down one night and had gone to sleep and had never woke up.

Beaver glanced around, noting how the neighborhood had changed. The frame houses seemed much smaller, more run-down and in need of painting. Junk cars lined the streets. As he walked past the park, he noticed a new baseball field and bleachers. The swimming pool fence was free from graffiti, but the ground around it was filled with unleveled terrain. The doors to the recreation center were chained and the place was closed.

When Beaver arrived in front of his old home, he suddenly felt as if he should turn and hurry away. The outside of the house was dirty and seemed more like a deserted shell that could crumble with one swift kick. He stood rooted to the grassless dirt beneath his feet, then glanced across at the old oak. The tree still grew strongly in the middle of the front yard. He went over to the tree and found his initials still carved deeply in the wood. Cande's were there, too. Seeing those initials made him feel sad, and with his finger he traced over them. Perhaps, he thought, they would recognize him.

He glanced at the door to the house, took a deep sigh, and went over. "Cande!" he called as he gently shoved open the unlocked door. There was no answer. The living room was vacant except for a sofa with ripped cushions. With the heels of his shoes echoing over the bare floor, he walked into the kitchen, kicking a beer bottle out of his way. Paper plates, plastic cups, empty milk cartons all littered the area. His mother's yellow formica table was still in the usual place. He unexpectedly yelled "Mama" then leaned against the kitchen sink, feeling sick to his stomach.

He suddenly got scared. What if Cande no longer lived here? He hurried to his brother's tiny bedroom and sighed with relief. Yes, he recognized the same sheets on his bed, Cande's old Ranger baseball cap, the sketches on the wall of low-rider cars, and an Aztec warrior. "Thank God!" Beaver cried.

Beaver went to his old room, which had been filled with poster girls and fancy cars. The girl posters were still there, but the car posters were gone. His bed was filled with wrinkled clothes, and there were unfamiliar things all around the room. His head hit a hanging light bulb, causing it to swing in circles. He reached up, steadied its movement, then switched it on. But it no longer worked. It needed a new bulb. Dump that the house was, he was thankful that it was a roof over their heads.

He thought of his father and his charming good looks. His father was tall and lean and could lie through his teeth and make everyone believe him. Nothing and no one was too good for his fast-money schemes. Papa liked to shock people by acting absolutely weird. He also loved the thrill of danger.

Beaver often wondered how the man managed to stay out of prison for burglary. He feared his father because of the beatings he'd inflicted upon him for years. At this moment, Beaver never wanted to see him again. He watched the light bulb swing back and forth. He took off his shoes, laid down on the mattress, and fell into an exhausted sleep.

Some time later, he awakened to a voice filled with surprise and wonder.

"Beaver, is that you?"

Beaver shook himself and opened his eyes. He shot up, not realizing where he was.

Cande stood next to him, unmoving. Slowly Cande smiled, watching as his older brother struggled to get out of bed and to this feet.

"Man, you're home at last," Cande said. His chest began to heave, and Beaver rushed to embrace him.

"I'm home for good, Cande." He held the thin boy an arm's length away. "Man, you're so tall and skinny! The first thing I'm going to do is go to the grocery store, get supplies, and cook us a good meal."

Cande stepped back from Beaver. "There's no money," he muttered.

"I've got a few bucks, so don't worry. I bet you didn't know that I was trained as a cook." Beaver looked at his brother's stooped shoulders and added, "I'm so glad to be home, Cande." He sat down on his bed, waited a moment to gather himself, then quickly pulled on his shoes.

Cande looked out the small frame window to the back yard. "I thought about you lots of times. Papa told me you'd never get out."

Beaver's eyes narrowed as if the old man had reached out and hit him once again. "I proved him wrong." Beaver shuffled through the old clothes that were thrown carelessly on his bed and found a blue bandana. Then he added, "You and I have always been a team, Cande."

"You know that Mama died. Papa promised me that he'd let you know that she'd died," Cande suddenly blurted out.

Beaver rose and went over to the cracked mirror that hung on the wall. There, he folded the bandana, put it to his forehead, and tied it into a tight knot at the back of his head. "Yeah, the chaplain told me about her death."

Beaver sighed deeply, not wanting to discuss it. "I felt bad at the time. That night, I had a dream that I was a little kid lost in a forest. The trunk of that tree was about six feet thick. Mama stood there waving her apron at me, and asking me to come closer. I got close enough to see the roses embroidered on her apron, and then I reached out for her hand and she smiled. A beam of light flooded down from the top of that old tree and we looked up. Only it was so bright that I had to cover my eyes with my hands. Finally, the light dimmed and I looked around. Mama was gone and so was the light.

"'Mama!' I screamed as I ran around the tree searching for her. I yelled her name many times, but she was gone. Finally, I woke up. I was in my bunk thinking that she looked peaceful in the dream and not suffering like she did here on earth. She's gone, but I think about her all the time, Cande."

Cande nodded, then blurted out, "Papa hurt everybody for no reason, Beaver. I hate him."

Cande stood facing the window, looking desolate as he sank deep into his own thoughts.

"He's a sick man, Cande. He can't help himself. All I know is that our mother is gone, but somehow she's watching over us."

Cande nodded slowly. "I wanted to go down to see you, but I didn't have the bus fare. I needed to talk to you real bad, especially after her funeral. Papa wouldn't give me the money. He claimed he had used all his money on her funeral. I did call the prison, but they told me you weren't allowed phone privileges."

Beaver stood silently for a moment, then said, "The thing that's important is that you tried." He touched Cande on his shoulder. "Let's go to the store. When we get back, we'll clean up the kitchen and I'll cook a fine meal." They walked out the front door.

"Cande, is Sundown Market still open?"

"Sure it is." They closed the front door, then Cande asked, "When did you learn how to cook, Beaver?"

"In prison everyone is assigned a job. I got put in the kitchen. At first I helped the cooks, like an assistant. I hated it, but I learned fast and worked my way up to being an assistant chef. I baked cakes, pies, and then cooked the main dishes." Beaver laughed. "I finally learned to eat vegetables. Mama would have been proud of me."

Cande managed a chuckle and Beaver glanced over at him. It was good to hear him laugh. "I'll bake a cake for us tonight so we can celebrate being team again."

"That's be great, Beaver."

"All the prisoners loved my pastries. They took to being nice to me so that they could get an extra dessert or an extra helping of whatever else there was. It was then that I learned I had a bargaining tool. If I needed a favor from them, I would save them an extra helping. You know, Cande...it's like

I'll scratch your back if you do this for me. It wasn't a bad thing and it sure helped me survive that hell-hole."

Cande only nodded in reply as they continued walking down the street.

Finally, Beaver asked, "Hey, Cande, tell me about school."

Cande glanced up at his brother as if he'd just been boxed across the ears. He stared at the tree-tops, then shrugged. "School is okay, Beaver."

"Okay, huh? What grade are you in now?"

"Ninth. I go to Pinkerton High."

"Do you have a girlfriend?"

"No!" Cande turned red in the face and stuck his hands in the pockets of his jeans."

"Do you know where Papa is?"

Cande's chin quivered as he looked up to the clouds. Then he answered. "He lives in Oak Cliff with some lady. He comes to the house every now and then."

Beaver angrily kicked a soft-drink can off the sidewalk.

"So, you don't see him much. Maybe it's best, Cande. He never was a good father. He doesn't give a fried bean about you or me!" Beaver saw Cande visibly shiver and instantly reached out to put his arm across his brother's shoulder.

"Are you okay?" he asked.

Cande nodded, studying the cracks on the side-walk.

The rest of the way to the market, they walked in silence. Beaver noticed that Cande seemed to withdraw like a turtle frightened of being seen or heard. Things had been rough for him, too.

On the parking lot outside the market, Beaver saw Pete, the homeless man who claimed the area as his territory for hustling. Everyone in the barrio knew better than to trespass into Pete's territory with drugs, and the prostitutes steered clear for fear of retaliation from old Pete. Even in his sixties, Pete could still do some damage to the young guys.

Beaver noticed old Pete had lost about twenty pounds and didn't look as fierce as he had when Beaver was younger. Pete was slouched against the phone booth near the entrance of the store. He flicked his cigarette to the ground and grinned. "Hey! I remember you!"

Beaver waved and walked up to him. Cande, not wanting to associated with old Pete, hung back several feet. "Pete, I can't believe you're still alive, man. You've got to be more than a century old!" Beaver added jokingly.

Pete straightened up proudly and quickly ran his dirty, tobacco-stained fingers through his gray hair. "I ain't seen you around for a long time, but I remember you. Did you move to Oak Cliff?"

"No, Pete." Beaver pointed to his burr haircut and said in a hushed voice, "I was in jail in Huntsville."

Pete smiled. "That's right! I bet you got yourself some good tips while in prison." He looked down at his worn boots. "I spent some time there, too. I believe I was about your age. Young and stupid!" He roared, then slapped Beaver on the shoulder.

Not wanting to talk about his prison stay, Beaver asked, "What's the news around here?"

"Usual stuff." He glanced over Cande, who pretended to toy with the soft-drink machine. "Got a smoke?"

"Sure, Pete." Beaver quickly handed him a cigarette and his book of matches. He watched Pete inhale and exhale slowly, as if this moment mattered more to him than his whole life. The old man's head fell forward a couple of times as if he couldn't hold it up anymore.

"You shooting dope, Pete?" Beaver questioned.

The stubble on old Pete's chin became stiff as he responded a bit angrily, "I steer away from that stuff, but there's plenty for the asking...if that's what you want." He glanced over at Cande again.

"No, thanks. What else do you know, Pete?"

"Oh, hot checks floating around the barrio. Company checks...fresh and blank, too. I don't mess with that either."

"Who's writing them?"

"Local guys."

"What's the figure they're writing?"

Pete grinned, "I hear two- to five-hundred dollars."

"Yep, that's big time in prison!" Beaver gasped.

"Yeah, but you know." Pete pointed his finger at Beaver as if he knew all there was to know in the world and was going to teach Beaver a lesson or two. "I ain't got the guts to go through with cashing them. But, if that's your game, I can lead you to the man. All you need is a nice suit and a fake identification card, and that's not hard to find in these parts. Just remember, the police always get you in the end."

Beaver glanced nervously at Cande, who leaned against the coke machine trying to be patient and pretending not to hear a word. "No," Beaver decided. "I'm staying clean."

"Got some smarts now. But, by God, there's nothing like sunshine and the great outdoors." He stood straighter. "Excuse me." He walked out to a car that had just driven up and leaned against the door to talk to someone.

Beaver motioned for Cande to follow him into the grocery store.

Cande immediately said, "Beaver, don't listen to old Pete! You know he's crazy."

Beaver pulled out a grocery cart. "In some ways Pete is crazy, Cande. But he knows what's happening in the barrio. It's like he's the main reporter around here, and what better way for me to catch up on the latest news?"

"Beaver, he'll get you in trouble!"

Beaver sacked several tomatoes and turned to Cande, "I learned the hard way how to take care of myself. Now, I'm taking care of you. So, don't worry, Cande."

Cande seemed relieved and didn't say much as they completed their shopping. Beaver paid for the groceries with the money they'd given him in prison. As they exited the store, old Pete was still by the telephone waiting. "Pete, do you know where I can find work?"

"Try the tire shop," Pete answered.

"Take care." Beaver shook his hand.

Old Pete nodded and smiled. "Hey, my parking lot is yours anytime."

"I'll remember that, Pete. Thanks."

As they carried the groceries home, Beaver asked Cande, "What do you eat at school?"

"I get my lunch free. Sometimes I buy a Coke and chips."

"I'm guessing you don't use your meal ticket. Maybe you're ashamed. Is that why you're hanging your head like you used to do whenever I got angry and yelled at you?"

"What difference does it make, Beaver? It's my stomach!" Cande hastily added. "I do all right."

"It makes plenty of difference, but it's okay. I'm home and I intend to fatten you up. All you have to do is make good grades."

Cande laughed. "I like art."

"I remember art was fun. You any good at drawing?"

Cande nodded and his eyes grew bright. "I like painting and sketching best. But paints and canvas are expensive. I mostly borrow from the other kids in the class to get my projects finished."

"After we eat, you can show me some of your work. Okay?"

Cande smiled nervously. "I don't like to show anyone my work."

"Why? You should be proud that you have a talent."

"Papa calls me a sissy, because I like to paint."

"What does Papa know!"

Once home, Beaver left the groceries in the sack while he asked Cande to pick up the trash that littered the kitchen. Beaver thought Cande would give him a hard time, but instead Cande worked hard and put the litter into one big bag. While his brother was busy, Beaver threw away a bunch of old plastic cups that were piled in the sink. "Hey, Cande, how come it's so messy here?"

Cande glanced at Beaver. "Sometimes Papa has parties and they make a mess. I leave the house and wait next door until his people are all gone."

Beaver cringed. "I see." He started peeling and chopping the potatoes. The thought of the old man using the place for wild parties made him angry. He sighed and shook his head, knowing there was nothing he could do about it...at least not right now.

After Cande had finished sweeping the floor, he sat on a chair and watched his brother. "Beaver, you've changed."

Beaver laughed. "So they tell me. You think it's good or bad?"

Cande shrugged. "At least you're home."

CHAPTER THREE

Supper was a joyful celebration. Beaver and Cande spent the time getting reacquainted. And even though Beaver did most of the talking, by the time he got up to slice the warm cake he'd baked, he had Cande laughing a lot. Judging from the amount of food that Cande ate, Beaver concluded his brother had not had a good meal in a while.

"Okay, Cande. It's time to see those paintings."

Cande's grin faded into a mixture of hesitancy and fear. Finally he said, "Beaver, promise that you won't laugh." He slowly rose and turned toward the hallway.

Beaver stood up, too. "I promise, Cande."

As Cande walked to his room, Beaver wanted to pat his brother's drooping shoulders to give him confidence. From the way Cande walked, it seemed he had an iron chain and ball welded on each leg. Beaver sat on Cande's bed while his brother rummaged through a few items in the closet.

"Remember," Cande said apologetically, "some of these are class projects."

"No problem," Beaver replied. "I used to like art myself, even though I wasn't much good at it."

Cande pulled out six canvases. "Close your eyes until I can arrange them."

Beaver turned his back. They're probably nudes, he thought. He found himself forcing back a laugh.

Cande braced the paintings across the base of the floor. After a few moments, he said, "You can look, now."

Beaver glanced down at the paintings, cleared his throat, then whistled slowly. He fell to his knees to study each canvas. The larger canvas was covered with bright flowers painted in rainbow hues. Another was of an old barn in an open meadow that was covered with miniature bluebonnets. One was of a priest in brown robes who walked alongside his donkey as they ambled around a mountain's edge. Beaver especially liked the painting of an Aztec god who sat regally upon his throne at the top of his pyramid. He studied the Aztec god's stern facial features. He could see the pain and suffering Cande had painted on his face.

Cande stepped closer, disrupting Beaver's thoughts. "Little Brother...I'm speechless." Beaver spread his arms to encompass all the paintings. "You've got talent! I had no idea! When did you start painting?"

"I started when Mama got sick. I didn't want to leave her alone, so I stayed home and painted. It helped pass the time for me. Then last summer, this Chicano artist named Carlos came to the center to paint a mural for the gym wall. He gave me lessons and some acrylic paints because I helped him paint the wall. After Carlos' project was over, he gave me a roll of canvas. He's a great artist. Carlos went to college to learn to paint like a pro! I want to be like him."

Beaver whistled loudly to show how impressed he was with Cande's talent as a painter. "Cande, my brother, the famous artist!" Beaver turned to view the room. "Where do you paint?"

"Outside on the back porch. It's too dark inside. Besides, no one can see me back there."

"I understand." Beaver watched Cande as he carefully gathered his work to store it away once again.

"I got 'Best-in-the-School-Art-Show' for this painting." Cande pointed to the wooden cabin surrounded by bluebonnets.

"I can see why! It's as if you could almost pick those bluebonnets. Cande, why don't you hang your pictures on your wall? They're cool!"

Cande hesitated, but finally answered, "I could...only..." He shook his head. "I'd best put them away."

"Why?"

"Because Papa might come in drunk and kick them."

"What!" Beaver said, aghast.

"Never mind. I'll put them away, Beaver... never mind. It'd be better if they are safely stored."

Beaver was alarmed by Cande's response and could sense that his brother was scared.

He said softly, "Cande, I'm home now. If you want to paint...you paint. You don't have to hide anything anymore. Okay?"

Cande stood up straight. "I'm glad you're home. Can I help you clean up your room now?"

Beaver smiled. "Sure. Come to think of it, I'm kind of tired and it's late. Let's do that tomorrow. While you're in school, I'll tackle the rest of the house." He gently touched Cande's shoulder then said, "I'll be here when you get home from school tomorrow."

"Great, Beaver. Maybe, we can go to the park."

"Sure, Cande."

The next afternoon Cande and Beaver cut across the unleveled terrain that was supposed to be a city-maintained soccer field. It was almost five in the afternoon and the sun was gently falling on what had been a beautiful spring day. They made their way around the pool compound, throwing jabs and punches at each other as they told each other funny jokes. Cande was genuinely happy to have Beaver home.

The recreation center was open and they pulled open the door in unison. Not too many kids were around at that hour, but in the weight room Beaver found Tony going through his workout.

Beaver laughed as he shook Tony's hand. "Tony! It's good to see you. Some people never change."

Tony took Beaver's outstretched hand and gripped it in a power hold that made Beaver flinch. Tony was twenty-eight, but because he was physically small and wore his wiry hair long, he looked much younger. He was street smart and quick at opening locked doors. He could go in and out of a house without making noise or leaving the slightest evidence that the house had been broken into. Yet, he kept his nose clean, and he'd be the first to admit that he did things the crazy way. Tony was also the best basketball player in the area and was team captain for the Lobos.

Beaver handed Tony a weight and watched him adjust the bar, wanting desperately to ask him a ton of questions about what had been happening in the barrio. But Beaver hesitated because he didn't know how Tony would accept his reappearance. The protocol of the barrio was that Tony was the leader. So Beaver just waited as he watched Tony lift the weights.

Tony pointed to another smaller weight, expecting Beaver to hand it to him. "Beaver, I gotta tell you, the barrio missed your presence."

Beaver signed in relief as Cande handed him a can of Coke. "Tony, I have to admit that I don't miss a thing about prison."

Tony stopped working out and eyed Beaver coldly. "Well, as I recall there was a few things I liked about being in prison."

Beaver fidgeted. "Yeah, I liked having three meals a day and I liked it when beer was smuggled inside. What I didn't like was having to buy it. Prison beer is expensive, and I didn't have the money to buy it."

That pleased Tony and he grinned. "I bet a party could bring back that beer taste." He lifted another weight and grunted. "What you need is a welcome back party. Yeah! A party with all your old friends together!"

Beaver glanced at Cande, then decided he'd best say something to acknowledge Tony's offer. "Yeah, a party sounds great!"

"By the way, have you seen Margie?"

Beaver felt as if Tony had thrown a bucket of ice at him. "No, I haven't seen her."

"Maybe you don't want to see her. Is that it?" Tony asked maliciously.

"It ain't nothing like that. It's just that I need time to get my head on straight. And," he glanced up at Cande, "there's still Cande to get used to. Plus, tomorrow I've got to report to this probation officer for the first time. I think I've got enough to deal with for right now."

Tony laughed, then clapped Beaver on the back. "Sounds like you've become a businessman or something."

Beaver nodded and pushed his bandana a little higher on his forehead. "Listen, Tony. I've got to go. I'll be checking with you real soon." He turned, left the weight room and walked toward the office, look-ing for the manager of the center, the man everyone in the barrio called Joe Columbus. Joe Columbus, from the Seminole Tribe in the state of Oklahoma, had just about raised Beaver and Cande.

Columbus was a big, sun-bronzed man. He'd look straight at you when he spoke to you and you'd wonder if he'd discovered your most buried secrets. He loved to coach basketball, and the kids in the barrio could count on him not to snitch to the police or to their parents as long as they didn't cause him problems.

Beaver stopped to look at the large terra-cotta mural that hung in the hallway. He searched it for the square he'd carved and glazed when he was ten-years old. It was still there: his own handprint with his name engraved across the length of the thumb.

Suddenly, a pair of strong arms wrapped snugly around Beaver's throat.

"Guess who?"

Beaver was lifted off the floor. He began kicking and realized it was Joe Columbus. "Hey, man! Put me down!" he begged.

Columbus promptly dropped Beaver as quickly as he'd lifted him. "Beaver!" he said happily. "Glad you're back home!" Joe Columbus held out his hand for Beaver to shake. His broad smile showed white teeth; his skin was as sun-bronzed and tough as ever.

Beaver gripped Joe Columbus' hand tightly and shook it.

Feeling like a midget next to Columbus' enormous physique, he did not see pity in his friend's brown eyes. Instead, Beaver saw a genuine concern.

Yes, he had missed this man more than anyone, except his mother and Cande. He laughed nervously on being caught exposing his emotions. "Hey, man. I thought you were supposed to be on a diet?"

Joe Columbus laughed so loudly that the echo of his laughter ran up and down the hallway. "I'm never on a diet. But I see you really lost a few pounds." He playfully boxed on Beaver's shoulder. "Learned how to box yet? You might develop some muscle structure!"

Beaver shook his head. "I don't like boxing!"

"Tony's got a good basketball team... you gonna join? You used to play on our teams!"

"I played basketball in prison and got to be a pretty tough player. I also got into jogging!"

"Well, you should be in shape. Come over Saturday morning for the first game and watch Tony's team. We're playing a church-league team from Oak Cliff."

Beaver nodded. "Sure, I will... if I can get up that early."

"There should be no problem, man. I hear they get you up at 5 a.m. in prison. Isn't that the truth?"

"It's true."

Columbus immediately noticed Beaver's frown and stood quietly observing the young man as he always used to do when Beaver was younger.

"How old are you?" Beaver asked as they walked toward Columbus' office.

"Beaver, I'm ancient at forty-nine, but I can still outrun your butt!" He laughed, then continued,

"I've been working here for a long time," he said as he fiddled with his keys. "I'm getting old and I'll probably be buried behind first base.

"Seriously though, the problem is the big guys up at City Hall who don't seem to pay attention to this park or my work. I shouldn't complain. At least I've got plenty of basketballs and a few good guys."

Beaver nodded that he understood. The big man suddenly reached over and put his large hand on Beaver's shoulder. "I know what you sacrificed, Beaver. You did what was right and Cande is the better for it. You're a real man, Beaver. Let me be the first to tell you that."

Beaver gazed out the glass window toward the baseball field. Perhaps Joe Columbus could understand a little of what he went through in prison, but Beaver didn't think anyone in the world could. Beaver whispered, "It was rough going. I thought I'd die, but somehow I didn't."

Columbus answered, "You died, but you didn't die. You're like the trees that die in winter, but in the spring they bloom once again. I like trees, Beaver. They're strong and everlasting." Joe Columbus was known for making people feel whole when their guts had been cut out and they were left bleeding.

"Beaver," he added, "I thought about you every day. I prayed for you at the end of each day, that you'd come out your old self. But I see you've changed. You were forced to change. Prison killed your spirit, but you're still breathing and eating, and that's good." He pointed to his heart and in a peculiar way ran his thumb across it as if he were playing the delicate strings of a guitar. "You're a true spirit, Beaver. So, live for the moment, forget about yesterday. Free yourself of that time...never look back. Go forward, I always say!"

Beaver glanced at Joe Columbus as he gently laid his huge hand over his heart in such a tender manner that Beaver knew he was offering him a token of peace. Beaver was touched and quickly glanced away. "Thanks, Joe," Beaver whispered, but his friend didn't hear him because he was busy blowing his whistle at some rowdy kids in the gym.

That evening, Beaver and Cande walked home from the park at eight. Cande talked about Carlos. He told Beaver about the way he dressed, how all he ever wore were blue-jean coveralls splattered with different colors of paint. "Carlos explained to me that each drop of paint on his coveralls reminded him of one of his completed projects." Cande shook his head in fascination.

"Well, if this Carlos is doing so well, how come he had to paint a mural in West Dallas? I mean, it's not like the rich people are going to see it. As a matter of fact, except for Joe Columbus and the Ledbetter kids, nobody will see it." As soon as Beaver said that, he wished he could withdraw the question. He had challenged his brother's newest hero and it had hurt Cande's feeling.

Cande walked along quietly for a few steps then stopped in his tracks. "Beaver, Carlos did the mural because he was raised here in West Dallas. He said he wanted to give something back to the community. He's got money; I've seen his house and his studio. He doesn't need to be anything other than himself."

"That's good. The guy is doing something he wants to do and, in my book, that's about the best you can be." Beaver quickly responded, hoping to erase any negative idea he might have projected toward Carlos.

Cande smiled. He was happy once again. It took so little to make Cande happy, and Beaver marveled at what the simplest stroke of kindness could produce. Cande was so young and fragile—that worried Beaver.

They walked in silence the rest of the way home. Beaver was thinking about meeting his probation officer the next morning. It was going to be rough and it was going to be another reminder of the three years of his life that had been wasted. He glanced down at his watch. Back in prison he'd be waiting for everyone to finish with the showers so he could take a quick one before they locked him in for the night. Afterwards, he'd lie on his cot for hours listening to the other guys toss and turn or call out in their sleep. Beaver pulled off his bandana from around his forehead and quickly ran his hand through his short hair. Just thinking about prison made him break out in a sweat. His Lady was tingling on his back. "Let's take a short-cut,

Cande," he said, pointing toward a tree in the center of a lot covered with knee-high weeds.

"No, Beaver!" Cande warned, grabbing his arm to stop him. "It's not safe to go through there."

The high shrill of Cande's voice alarmed Beaver, and he quickly glanced behind him and then over toward the lot. It didn't seem dangerous to him, but Cande was shaking. "Okay, Cande. We'll go the long way." They walked on and Beaver glanced over his shoulder once again at the lot, wondering what frightened Cande so much.

CHAPTER FOUR

The crisp morning air refreshed Beaver, and the smell of fresh Mexican pastries which baked in Mr. Garza's Bakery made his stomach rumble. He wanted to rush inside the shop to buy a piece of delicious bread and a cup of coffee, but he was afraid that he'd miss his bus. He didn't want to be late for his first meeting with his probation officer. Reluctantly, Beaver decided to walk on toward the corner bus stop. There he turned his attention to the limping old man who helped the kids safely cross the street in order to attend the nearby elementary school. The man seemed familiar to Beaver, who paced back and forth jingling change in his pockets as he glanced down Singleton Boulevard searching for a glimpse of the Ledbetter bus.

"Going into town?" asked the guard when he reached Beaver's side of the busy street.

Beaver nodded and glanced at the guard's neon orange vest and flag that aided him in doing his work.

"The bus is usually about five minutes late every morning. It's been that late since I started this job." He looked seriously at Beaver's hair. "You should wear a hat. Somedays the breeze blows hard here. Other days, it fills our lungs with dust or stench from the dump." He scratched the back of his neck. "Say, don't I know you?" He looked directly at Beaver's eyes. "Maybe, I know your Papa?"

Beaver moved away from him, but the guard continued to study him. "No!" Beaver insisted while he kept his eyes averted. Beaver stood taller than the guard, who wiped his bald head with a bandana, then proceeded to cross the street to help a group of kids cross the intersection.

The man's stare made Beaver uneasy. Still the bus did not come and Beaver was getting upset. Before he knew it, the guard stood before him and stated, "You look familiar, but you know, I see so many people every day. No matter. I'm Conrado Martín. Maybe you've heard of me. I'm president of the Barrio Association. Maybe you or your parents would like to join our association. We help with projects that make the barrio a better place to live."

"No, thanks," Beaver replied. The bus pulled up right in front of where Beaver stood and he quickly boarded, leaving Mr. Martín to assist the kids that crossed the busy intersection. Beaver watched him from the bus window, thinking Mr. Martín shouldn't be talking so much nor should he be so trusting of strangers. Beaver could well imagine a thug stabbing him or mugging him right on the spot. Old people shouldn't be so friendly, Beaver thought. From associating with criminals in prison, Beaver knew for a fact that no one in the real world was ever safe from those mean characters. Senior citizens, in particular, were targeted by criminals.

Beaver arrived downtown, and from his wallet he pulled out the business card with the name C. Rodríguez printed on it. Beaver rubbed his sweaty palms together. He was definitely nervous about this first meeting with his new probation officer. He hesitated a minute outside the office doors to gather his wits. He really didn't know what to expect nor how to act with a probation officer. In prison, he was told what to do and when to do it, but out here he never knew what was coming down.

The office reminded him of the principal's office in an antiquated elementary school. It had heavy, old wooden furniture that would take two guys to move. The windows looked frosted, but on closer inspection he saw that they were painted over. The whole place smelled musty and damp. He approached the front desk and waited for the lady to notice that he was standing there. He shuffled his feet together and she immediately turned.

"Oh, can I help you?" she asked as she approached the counter where Beaver stood.

Beaver leaned on the counter and asked, "I need to see this person." He handed her the card he had held clutched tightly in his hand.

She smiled. "Well, you're going to have to wait a while. Rodríguez is due any minute. Have a seat."

Beaver moved to the chair that fit snugly in a corner near a table loaded with magazines. He seated himself, then picked up one of the magazines and leafed through it. He waited more than an hour.

The receptionist finally called him. "Rodríguez is here. Follow me, please."

He followed her down the hallway to an office door where she stopped and pointed.

"Go right in," she said. Beaver nodded a thank you, went in, and quickly surveyed the office. The desk was stacked with files. A brown-bag lunch sat on top of the files, a radio was faintly playing, and an unopened umbrella was standing in the trash can. He noticed a name plate embossed with the name C. Rodríguez. He had just decided to sit down when a woman appeared at the door.

"Hello. I'm Cookie Rodríguez. Sorry to keep you waiting." She walked past Beaver and he stood speechless. She didn't wait for him to sit down before she began searching her desk for a file folder.

"I know who you are. Francisco Torres, right? One of the notorious Torres's of Ledbetter. I know all about your family from police officers in West Dallas." She continued to flip through the stack of files.

Beaver was speechless. "You're a woman!" he suddenly found himself screaming at her.

She stopped and glared up at him. "You noticed, but don't let that bother you, because I'm one of the best in this field." Her voice was harsh and she smiled like an army sergeant who had just won a brawl and enjoyed it immensely.

"So, Francisco, let's get down to business."

"Look, lady," Beaver added, "this is a big mistake! I want a man probation officer!"

She stared at him and then answered, "I see… You want a man as your probation officer. Presently, the men we do have on staff deal with hard-core cases like rapists and murderers." She pointed to the chair indicating that he should sit.

Beaver flopped down dejectedly into the chair. He should have expected this, he told himself, because his luck ran reverse of what he wanted. He was not prepared for this woman with shoulder-length auburn hair who was dressed professionally in a navy suit. To top it off, she had fiery hazel eyes. She looked around twenty-eight, perhaps no older than thirty, he decided. She looked like the type woman one would expect to see in a fine department store selling expensive perfumes. Her large eyes definitely narrowed when she spoke.

"Plant this fact into your head," she said. "The next time you're caught doing something illegal, the court will not go easy on you."

"Yeah," Beaver answered angrily as he clutched and opened his fists in an effort to calm himself. "I know what will happen to me if I go back to prison. I learned a lot of things in prison, lady."

Her stare remained cold and unimpressed. She was not disturbed by what he said. Yet she continued to stare boldly at him until she forced him to look away. He leaned forward, resting his elbows on his knees, studying the pattern of the floor tiles and shaking his head at this unlucky turn of events.

"My advice to you is to get a job as soon as possible. Get away from the friends who helped you get in trouble in the first place."

She found his file, scanned it, then summarized what she had read. "It was a friend who got you in trouble—Mingo Alvárez. Mingo and you held up the Jack-in-the-Box. Mingo terrorized the woman teller at the drive-in, but she identified him as the one with the gun. She didn't get a good look at you. During the interrogation, Mingo pointed the finger naming you as his companion. Says here...you were the 'silent partner.' Some of the witnesses from a car that was behind Mingo's said that there was a third party in the back seat, but no identification was made on him or her. The person in the car parked directly behind Mingo's got the license number." She was quiet for a moment as if turning things over in her mind, trying to sort things out.

Beaver wanted to spring across the desk and choke her, but he did nothing and said nothing, even though his rage was mounting. He willed his concentration on the pattern of floor tiles, daring not to look up at her.

"Mingo would not tell who that person in the back seat was, nor did you tell," she added, then quickly threw down the folder. "Yet, it was obviously someone you both knew. What kind of deal did you and Mingo work out?"

Beaver jumped up in anger. "We didn't cut a deal!"

Just as quickly, she jumped out of her chair, too. "Sure, Francisco... No deals! I'd bet you're covering for someone. Maybe one of your girlfriends, Francisco?"

"You're guessing, lady! You don't have a finger of proof!" He turned away and stared out the window.

She continued. Her voice commanded his attention. "Move to a different area of town or a different neighborhood. Start over where no one knows about your past. As I see it, Francisco, you've got two strikes against you now. One is your father and the other is your prison background."

"What do you know about me or my father?!" Beaver yelled, incensed.

"I know enough about both of you. Just remember, Beaver, that trouble brews trouble. So don't get involved with guns, drugs, prostitutes, theft or anything that looks suspicious or shady."

"My life is mine to do with as I please. No one is going to tell me what to do!"

She smiled knowingly. "Oh, yes, Francisco. I'll not only tell you what to do, but I'll tell you what is expected of you. Plan on visiting me weekly here at this office. You don't know when I'll be around checking you out. If I so much as catch you out of bounds, then I'll pull you in so fast that it will leave you breathless... at which time the real game between me and you and the law starts." She stared at Beaver a long time, making sure her facts soaked into his head.

Suddenly she turned her chair to stare at a painting of a deep blue sea that hung on the opposite wall. It seemed to calm her.

"Francisco, look here. If you need help with a new place to stay, there are halfway houses. I could find you a cheap apartment. I'll find you a job. You work with me and I'll work with you."

"Rodríguez, I have a place to stay. So stay away from me unless it's necessary, and I'll work hard to keep out of your way." Beaver stood up to leave the office.

Rodríguez held out her card. "I can be reached at this number any hour of the day... Use it," she advised, not bothering to get up from her chair. "See you next Friday, 9 a.m. sharp." She stared at Beaver directly. "Francisco, the time to change is now."

"Sure, Ms. Cookie Rodríguez." Beaver stopped at the doorway and turned to ask one last question. "Are you married?"

"That's none of your business!" she snapped hastily. "Your business is to keep your nose clean."

"Just wondering if some guy would be dumb enough to have such a hard-nosed cookie like yourself as his girl!" Beaver turned and left the office, slamming the door behind him.

He walked as fast as he could away from the office, hurrying around busy street corners of downtown Dallas, not even seeing people because he was so fired-up mad. He finally stopped at a coffee shop and went in for a sandwich. He was served fast and ate quickly. It wasn't until he'd had his third cup of coffee that he started to calm down and look around.

Outside the window of the coffee shop was a little park of concrete and grass. Tall trees graced its four corners and in the center a clump of spruce trees in various sizes grew tall and contrasted sharply with the concrete and glass buildings that surrounded the park. From where Beaver sat, the park seemed so peaceful and unusual. He rose and crossed the street to inspect it. He found an extremely tall man-made waterfall that sent water cascading over miniature steps. The bubbling sound was so pleasant that it soothed him. He sat on the edge of the waterfall for a long time, dipping his hand into the bubbling water, amazed by its coldness. People hurried out of tall office buildings with brown-bag lunches and sat on the velvet-green grass eating their lunches, talking, or just walking around. Beaver watched them with renewed interest. Those people were free. They were secretaries, bookkeepers and professionals all trying to complete the workday and get themselves home. Those people offered Beaver a glimpse of a life that years ago he would have thought was beyond his reach. As he studied them, he decided that he could be like them...if he wanted. He could be anything he wanted. Yes, he could be anything he wanted. He just needed the desire, but he had that, too. He had his G.E.D. and that meant he was a high school graduate...someone not standing on invisible air. He was someone with something to offer to the world. He just needed a chance, and he would find that opportunity.

The crowds thinned and he knew their lunch hours were over. He sat there and wondered where Ms. Cookie Rodríguez had her lunch. Then he saw a woman come out from behind the tall waterfall.

Puzzled, he moved closer and noticed three steps leading down to double doors. He decided to pull them open and found himself in a beautiful chapel. There were no windows in the circular chapel and the pews could not hold more than fifteen people. The hushed underground atmosphere was overwhelming. Beaver could hear the pounding of his heart. The carpet was thick and lush. The altar was bare and made of a white marble streaked with lines of gold. He decided to have a seat.

His mind wandered to that frightful night when Mingo held up the Jack-in-the-Box. Rodríguez had been right. There had been someone else in the back seat of the car. Cande had been in the passenger seat and Mingo drove the car that memorable night. It had been Mingo's idea to hold up the place. Beaver was exhausted from unloading a truck full of steel pipes that day, and that evening he'd attended a dance. After the dance he'd fallen asleep in the back seat of Mingo's car, thinking that they were going directly home. He had awakened to find Mingo driving at incredible speed and Cande yelling at him to stop. A gun lay between them alongside money that had been hastily thrown down on the seat. Beaver took the gun and forced Mingo to stop the car, then pulled Cande out. Beaver yelled at him to go home as he handed him a fistful of money.

"Go, Cande, go home! You don't know what happened to me after the dance. Do you hear! Keep your mouth shut no matter what. Promise me that, Cande." Beaver hurriedly hugged his brother while he steadily held the gun on Mingo.

Cande whimpered, "I promise, Beaver."

Beaver got back in the car, then forced Mingo to drive to a nearby park where he got out of the car. There, he pulled Mingo out and began beating him. Beaver told Mingo that if he spilt the beans that Cande was in the car with them, he'd kill Mingo no matter how many years it took or how many miles it took to find him. Beaver subtly reminded Mingo of his sister, who was Cande's age. "Hey chump! If you dare mention a word about Cande, your precious sister will die and then your widowed mother will die next!" Beaver meant every word of it. "And, piece of shit, if I get caught and can't get out of prison to do it, I've got people on the outside who can keep track of your family, particularly your little sister, until I'm available to finish the job!"

Mingo had believed Beaver and had never revealed that Cande had been in the car that night. As they took Mingo from the courtroom, he glanced at Beaver and nodded, meaning that he'd kept his mouth shut. Beaver had not smiled back at Mingo because the score between Mingo and himself was still unsettled. Mingo got fifteen years and Beaver was tried as an adult. As an accomplice, a partner in crime, Beaver was sentenced to ten years.

In this serene chapel, so much like he imagined heaven should be, Beaver could not hold back his tears. He knew he shed them for all the suffering he'd endured while in prison, and as he relived all the frightening moments of the trial, he remembered the sight of his mother sitting there behind him with her head bowed to her chest as if deeply shamed. He remembered seeing how Cande's head hung even lower. All that had been punishment enough, but he kept his mouth shut for Cande's sake. Mama would have surely died if she'd known that Cande had been in the car as well. Mama died anyway, and Beaver never got the chance to tell her that he was innocent. Not that it mattered now, but he would have liked her to know that he had been clean.

He felt at that very moment that his mother sat there beside him. He could swear he heard her soft sigh. Beaver wished more than anything that he could lay his head upon her shoulder and be free of all that plagued him. Life, he knew, would never be simple again.

Beaver remained in the chapel all afternoon. He thought of the time Joe Columbus had bought him a nice watch simply because he wanted him to finish the school year with passing grades. He

smiled. Joe Columbus was really radical in the type
of things he chose to do, but he was into giving
away all that he had and that included tender lov-
ing care. Beaver finished the tenth grade only
because Joe Columbus asked him that favor.

Beaver finally walked out of the chapel and
into the dimming sunlight. He walked slowly out of
the park to the main street to catch the bus back to
Ledbetter. He was not in a rush to see anyone, nor
was he anxious to get home. At the corner he
stopped and glanced back at the park, as if freezing
the sight in his memory. He decided that the reason
he liked the little chapel so much was because there
was no chaplain, no priest, no rabbi present. It was
Beaver one-on-one with the Lord.

The bus stopped and he got off. Much to his
amazement, the street-crossing guard was back on
the corner helping the kids return home from
school.

"Hey, there!" the guard shouted, waving his red
flag at Beaver. "Are you interested in a job?" he
yelled as he hurried to catch up with him.

Beaver stopped and turned quickly. "Did you
say job?"

"Yes, I said a job!" Mr. Martín squinted his eyes
and looked directly at Beaver. "Wino Pete told me
that Jack Miller at the tire shop was looking for a
helper. It won't hurt to check it out, son. You look
like a strong healthy young man. I think you could
handle the work."

"I'll check it out. I got some experience as a chef, but right now I need some money fast...like this week."

Mr. Martín nodded that he understood. "Jack gives his jobs to West Dallas residents first. He always says that the people of West Dallas give him their tire business and he ought to give back to those people whenever he can manage it. Now, I know for a fact that he ain't no rich man, but he makes a fair living out of the tire business and he contributes to our community events. He's a good man." Martín turned to take some kids across the street. "Our next meeting is Thursday night at the recreation center. Try to make it!"

"Thanks!" Beaver yelled over the roar of the traffic.

Cande would be home from school soon and Beaver wanted to fix a simple supper for him. It was Friday, the end of a tough week. First thing he planned to do tomorrow was to see Mr. Miller about that job. He clutched the folded newspaper he'd found on the bus seat. Tonight after supper he was going to look in the want ads for a job as a chef. Dallas was full of restaurants, but the trick would be finding one close enough to home so he could ride the bus back and forth. Anyway, in a year or so he could save enough money to buy a car. With the help of his Lady, he'd do that.

CHAPTER FIVE

Beaver got out of bed early Saturday morning, dressed quickly, and walked hurriedly toward the tire shop. He was determined to find a job.

He was the man of the house. He was going to make sure Cande concentrated on his studies rather than worrying about his next meal. Beaver nervously lit a cigarette. He hated looking for jobs. As he passed Garza's Bakery, the smell of freshly cooked pastries and breads made him realize that he should have taken the time to eat something at the house, but he had not wanted to disturb Cande, who had been sleeping soundly when he'd peeked into his room. The aroma of spicy *empanadas* forced him to retrace his steps and enter the bakery. The stacks of *pan dulce* and *pan de huevo*—egg-batter bread—as well as other treats, all neatly placed in rows inside the glass counter, were irresistible. Beaver quickly pulled out a dollar for coffee and a sweet roll, then took his tray to a corner table to eat.

"Francisco, *¿eres tu*? Is it really you?"

Beaver swallowed his first bite of bread, then looked up to see Mr. Garza. Mr. Garza's shiny black hair, which Beaver had admired as a boy, was now silver. Garza had put on about fifty extra pounds since Beaver had last seen him, but his face was still bright with a pudgy smile that told everyone that the world was an excellent place to live in and that everything was for the best. "Señor Garza, ¡qué gusto!" Beaver rose out of respect and shook his hand.

"Francisco! How are you, son?" The older man sat opposite Beaver and studied his face intensely. "I'm glad you're home."

Beaver could feel himself turn red in the face. The whole barrio knew about his time in prison. He had to face that fact and learn to deal with his new identity as an ex-con. He chuckled nervously then said, "It was hard, Mr. Garza."

Garza nodded, "Yes, I can imagine. It must have been as hard as me loosing my son Andy. He died this spring of cancer. He was just twenty-four, Beaver…about your age. Bless his soul. You do remember him, don't you?"

"Sure, I remember him. He always sat in that far corner and stared out the window. It seemed to me that he was always daydreaming or reading a book. He always said hello to me. He was a smart guy. Didn't he attend the gifted and talented school?"

Garza smiled, pleased that Beaver remembered so much about Andy. "Yes, yes, and he finished one year of college, too, before that disease ate him up," Garza lamented with a deep sigh. "Yes, he was always looking out that window. One day I asked him what he was staring at and he said, 'My guardian angel, Papá. What else could be so breathtaking?'"

Beaver remained silent and then took a sip of his coffee, giving Garza time to get his feelings together.

"Guardian angel, ha! Do you believe in guardian angels, Beaver?" the man asked seriously. But before Beaver could reply, Garza added, "For me and you, it's time for a new start. Changes are always good, even though at times we don't think so. I remember when you would come in here every morning and after school with your dime or two and buy Cande and yourself a piece of bread. Remember that?"

Beaver merely nodded and sipped his coffee.

"Anyway," Garza continued, "I thought of you often while you were away. Your mother would come in once in a while, but I didn't have the heart to ask her anything about you. My wife told me your poor mother quit talking after you went to prison. After that, no one ever saw her. Bless her soul!"

After a respectable minute of silence, Beaver asked, "Mr. Garza, I'm looking for work. I gotta help Cande. The food stamps aren't enough."

The baker nodded that he understood as he rubbed his hands over his bushy eyebrows. "I'd hire you, Francisco, but just last week I hired another boy. But, I tell you what...if he doesn't work out, I'll let him go and you can work for me."

"I got some experience as a cook in prison. I can really drum up some business for you. One thing you might consider is a portable cook counter in order to sell tacos for breakfast and lunch."

"Good idea, Francisco. Say!" he snapped his fingers, "come to think of it, Jack at the tire shop was just here. He's had his coffee and bread here for the last twenty years. He's looking for a helper. Go see him, Francisco. I'll have Señora Gómez say a prayer to help you out."

Beaver quickly finished his sweet roll then added, "I'm going over to the tire shop right now. See you soon, and thanks for the prayer and all."

Beaver headed out in the crisp morning air and hurried the six blocks down Singleton Boulevard to Miller's Tire Shop. Jack Miller's blue Chevrolet truck was parked in front of the shop.

He went inside and shouted, "Hey, Jack!" Then he waited. The shop wasn't a clean place. Dirt and dust from years past were caked on the floor and cabinets. "Jack!" Beaver yelled out once again.

A door suddenly opened at the very rear of the shop and Jack ambled out. He had on mechanic overalls and greasy boots. A little over sixty-five years of age, Jack was well known in the barrio. He was not the type of guy to cheat you in business.

"Coming!" he shouted back at Beaver. "Hold your horses!"

He stopped before Beaver and stared at him for a long second before saying, "Oh, I remember you. Skunk or Beaver or something like that. Ain't seen you in a long while. Need a flat fixed?" he asked, taking a faded red bandana out of his rear pocket and wiping his wrinkled forehead.

"I need a job," Beaver said immediately. "And, I'll tell you right out, Jack, I've been in prison for the last three years."

Jack remained silent for a while as he studied Beaver, then said, "I heard about your ordeal, but you know, son, I've been in the community for many years. I ain't got awful much to sell or steal, and I'll give you a try to even out the debt to the folks I owe here in West Dallas."

"I'll work hard, Jack. I'll even make us a good lunch every day!"

"Hey! Hey! Lunch, too. You're a man after my soul. I haven't had a decent meal since my wife passed away five years ago." He wiped his face with his handkerchief once again. "Okay, son, but I need you today, right now, and if I catch you up to no good, then I'll let you go quicker than a rat trap snaps at a mouse. Let that be fair warning."

"Don't worry, Jack." Beaver reached out and shook the older man's hand. "You won't be sorry for hiring me."

"See those tires stacked in that corner. They need to be moved out back inside the chain-link fence. Those are the tires we exchanged from yesterday's business. You'll see, it gets real busy from around ten in the morning until four in the afternoon. I got a refrigerator and a cook stove in the little room behind the office. I also got a cot back there, but that's for me to use.

Aside from the five dollars per hour, I'll pitch in another ten dollars each day for meals…but that's if I like them. Is that a deal?"

Beaver smiled. "It's a good deal."

"Now get on with it. See me after you finish with those tires."

Beaver worked at one project after another until he stopped to fix lunch. Jack gave him some money to buy groceries, and he was off trotting to the Sundown Market. Beaver wanted to make some skillet corn bread and chili. It was a favorite dish of the guys in prison, and Beaver purposely made the chili very hot. He had discovered that the hotter he made it, the better the guys liked it. They soon labeled his chili "Beaver's Special Chili—Hot Enough To Blow Your Pants Off!"

It didn't take Beaver long to prepare lunch, and they ate it at Jack's cluttered desk. Beaver watched Jack's face closely as he took his first bite. There was no reaction until he'd taken his fifth bite, then his right eyebrow flew up and he turned red around the eyes and neck. But Jack didn't stop lifting that spoon to his mouth until he ate the last there was. Then he managed to say, "Beaver, you brought tears to my eyes and I appreciate that."

Beaver laughed, taking his comment as a compliment. "I'm glad you liked my chili, Jack. I've got another surprise for you at lunch tomorrow!"

"I think I'm going to enjoy having you around, son. Just throw everything in the trash and let's get back to work."

Promptly at six in the afternoon Jack yelled, "Quitting time, son. Close the chain-link gates and we'll get out of here." Jack headed to the men's room as Beaver pulled the ten-foot-tall gates closed, then wrapped a large chain around the center steel poles and padlocked them. Jack came out of the rest room. He'd washed and changed into clean clothes.

By the time Beaver got the grime off his hands, arms and elbows, he was bone tired. Cooking all day long was a lot easier than this type of work, but at least this was honest work. He enjoyed working with Jack, whose pace wasn't so much demanding as steady.

"Beaver," he said as he held out an envelope. "I went ahead and gave you a day's wages. You earned it. I also included lunch money for tomorrow. See you at nine in the morning."

"Thanks, Jack." Beaver took the envelope, folded it in half and stuck it in his pocket, then headed to the house.

As Beaver walked home, he decided that he'd stick it out with Jack until the hot weather hit. By then, he'd rather be working as a cook in some air-conditioned restaurant. He felt the envelope in his pocket. It felt good having $45 in cash.

Beaver couldn't wait to tell Cande about his luck today. He entered the house wondering how Cande's day had gone. His brother wasn't in his room. "Cande!" he called as he took off his dirty shirt and threw it on the floor.

"Out back!" Cande responded.

Beaver went out the back door and found him painting under the shade tree. Cande had propped the canvas in position by using a couple of two-by-fours which he had leaned at an angle against the tree. Nails held the canvas in place and a wooden fruit crate served as his stool. Beaver glanced over Cande's shoulder and saw that the boy was painting his mother's favorite rose bush. "I got lucky today, Cande. I started working with Jack at the tire shop."

Cande stopped painting and looked up at Beaver. "Serious?"

Beaver nodded. "Mr. Garza told me that Jack was looking for a helper and I went right over. But, the best thing is that Jack paid me a day's wages."

"Beaver! That's great!" Cande took the envelope and looked into it. "Man, he really did!"

"Yes, he did. I worked like a dog! I even cooked lunch for him. He liked my chili."

"Chili sounds good to me," he added.

A high-pitched happy voice suddenly called out. "¡Hola!"

Cande turned and glanced toward the fence. Beaver followed his gaze, then raised his arm to wave. "Hello, Mrs. Chavarría."

"Beaver!" she called, waving her arm for him to come closer. "It's good to see you're home. I will rest better since you'll be around to take care of that boy. He's like a beanpole...so skinny. Here." She handed Beaver a brown-paper lunch sack. "I made you some tortillas for your supper, Beaver."

Beaver reached over the cyclone fence and gladly took them. "They're fresh. I can smell them, Mrs. Chavarría. *Muchos gracias.*"

"Ah, Beaver. I'm glad you're back. Every day I worry about this one." Her gaze was steady on Cande. "He's a good boy. Your Mamá, bless her soul, raised two good boys and then put up with that terrible husband of her's, but he has no cause to be beating on Cande. I don't believe there was a time when he wasn't punching Cande in the stomach or in the face. The devil take that man! But you know what they say, the devil grants his people long lives so that they can continue their meanness and do harm to other innocents." She flapped her arms around hopelessly, then added, "We can't have everything." A surprised look crossed her face. "Ah, I almost forgot. Your Mamá left a letter for you. Wait here, Beaver."

Beaver stood at the fence, glancing back at Cande. He could feel the anger build up inside him. Cande had never told him about the beatings.

Shortly, the screen door opened and Mrs. Chavarría reappeared. She carried a small envelope and held it out to him. "Beaver, that father of yours usually comes by late Friday or Saturday night... You know, before he goes to those clubs. Most of the time he's already drunk. *Ay, Dios mío.* If you need any help, come over to my house."

"Tell me what else has been happening since I've been gone," Beaver added anxiously.

"He hurts Cande, so badly that it takes him a day or two before he's up and about. Poor boy. If that man comes by drunk, there will be a beating... Past experience tells me that!"

Beaver paled, swallowed hard, then moved closer. "Tell you what, *Señora*. We'll go out the back door when he comes through the front, but I'm not afraid of him," Beaver said bravely, even though his stomach pitched into a turmoil.

She rubbed her hands on her apron and stared silently at him before she added, "Look... I've known your family since the beginning of time. Your father is like he is because your grandfather was with the Mexican Mafia back in the old barrio days, and that gang did some pretty bad things in their time. Your father has always had a bad temper, but since your Mamá died, he's gone completely mad. I believe it's because he cannot sell this house. He wants quick money, and if he sells this house, it will bring him the quick money in one large chunk. You understand, don't you, that your Mamá left the house to Cande because you were in prison and there was no one else? I would not doubt that he would try to kill the boy to sell this house. The devil lives in that man!"

Beaver nodded. "We'll be all right. Don't worry, and thanks for the tortillas."

"Beaver, if you need anything, just call me." She turned and disappeared behind the screen door.

Beaver joined Cande. He was thankful that *Señora* Chavarría had always lived there and that they had more or less adopted her, but he was worried because at any time his father might show up. "Cande, let's get cleaned up and go out to eat. Hurry, man. This money is burning a hole in my pocket!" Beaver had a slight note of happiness in his voice. He picked up Cande's tubes of paint and took a moment to stare at the bright red roses Cande had painted on the canvas. Cande, he realized once again, was talented. "Brother, someday you're going to be a great artist and you'll never have to worry about money... or anything else again."

Cande only smiled as he continued to put the tops on his tubes of paint.

"Got any clean clothes to change into?" Beaver asked as he followed Cande into the house.

"Sure, Beaver. Mrs. Chavarría lets me use her washer whenever I want." He turned and entered his room. "You know, if it wasn't for her, I think I'd be dead."

"Is that so?" he softly commented, desperately wanting to question him about the beatings his father had inflicted upon him. But he also didn't want to put a damper on their supper plans. "Well, come on! Get in the shower." Beaver stood at the door to Cande's room. "By the way, how did you manage to keep the water on?"

Cande glanced up, then continued rummaging through some clothes. "I sold some of my food stamps." He sort of shrugged. "I preferred having the water on. I could always use candles at night, which was cheaper than paying for electricity."

"How did you get food stamps?" Beaver asked curiously.

"Mamá filled out the papers before she died. I just kept signing her name. Mr. Curtis at Sundown knew Mamá was sick, so he never asked questions."

Cande's shoulders hunched forward as if to acknowledge that he had done something illegal. Then he looked Beaver directly in the face. "It was all I could do. I had to eat!"

Beaver only nodded. "Hurry with your shower."

While Cande showered, Beaver sat on his bed and stared at the letter from his mother. He was afraid to open it. His mother was a person who didn't know where she was going, he thought. Her ideas were different and her thoughts were scrambled. Understanding her was a real problem for Beaver. In an effort to pacify Cande and Beaver after some brutal onslaught instigated by her husband, she would try to explain how she felt about their father. But the feeling she felt for him was too difficult for her to explain, and she never managed to untangle her thoughts and to get the boys to understand their father. Then frustration would cause her to clam up and she would dismiss the issue. Not being a person who liked reading or writing, she could not write her thoughts down in a letter, either.

He listened a second to make sure Cande was busy with his shower before he slowly opened the letter.

Beaver, she wrote. Not Dear Beaver, but simply Beaver. I'm sick. Since you've been gone to prison, it's worse. I know I'll die, but for me that is not so bad. For Cande and you, it will be bad. I could protect both of you from your father a little longer, but I do not have the strength. He doesn't care what he does to us and he never will. I know that now. I have left the house to Cande. When you leave prison, you and Cande can stay together here in my house. I wanted to leave it to you, but I was afraid since you were in prison he could take it away and sell it. *Señora* Chavarría has a copy of the deed to the house. I told her to keep it and hide it. Cande does not know about this. Mr. Soto, the attorney, has the original deed. When you get a chance, go see him. I do not believe that you robbed that Jack-In-The-Box. When you come out, try to be happy. Life is much too short not to be happy. Find someone who really loves you. Promise to take care of Cande. Your mother, Marta Torres.

Beaver's heart felt heavy. Mamá had done her best to cope with a bad situation, and he could not fault her. He wanted her to forget all the bad things that had happened to her in her lifetime. He wanted her to sleep peacefully...something she had never been able to do on this earth. He closed his eyes a moment and could see her standing before him, smiling at him as if she had a joke to tell him, then quickly running her hand through his hair.

He carefully folded the letter and put it back inside the envelope, then began searching for a safe place to hide it. He decided it was best to tear it into a million pieces and trash it. No sooner had he finished doing that than Cande came out of the shower.

"Where we going to eat?" Cande asked as he entered his room.

"We'll follow the road, Cande," Beaver replied as he entered the bathroom.

"Sounds like an adventure."

"Cande, our life has always been an adventure, hasn't it?"

Cande only laughed.

Beaver showered and dressed quickly. He took the envelope with his wages then joined Cande, who stood on the porch waiting. Beaver closed the front door. "Well, we're off on our new adventure." He put his arm over Cande's shoulder and they hurried down the block. Beaver kept glancing back toward the house. No car drove up. So, at least for this Friday night, they had escaped.

They didn't have to wait long at the bus stop. They boarded and picked a seat. Beaver was glad they had missed an encounter with his father. He also felt a special thanks for Ms. Chavarría.

"You know, Cande, I'm gonna buy Ms. Chavarría a rose."

A puzzled look crossed Cande's face. "Why, Beaver? There's plenty of roses in our back yard. She can have all she wants."

Beaver nodded, "That's right. Then, I'll buy her some candy."

"Why buy her anything? It's not her birthday. I know her birthday is in August."

"Because," Beaver added, "she looked after you while I was gone."

Cande looked down at the rail in front of him. "She's a nice lady. I gave her a painting of a pink flamingo for her last birthday. It's in her living room. You're right, she was always there when I needed her and when Mamá needed her."

"She's a good woman, Cande," Beaver said, noticing that Cande had turned to concentrate on the buildings the bus passed. He is so different, Beaver thought to himself. He has so many of Mamá's ways.

They got off the bus and entered the Nopalito Restaurant, a Mexican restaurant off McKinney Avenue. The table they selected was in a semi-dark corner where the two could easily watch the people come and go. After the meal, they began talking of all the things they had done as kids.

"Beaver, let's come here every Friday night. This is the most fun I've had in a long time."

Beaver eagerly nodded. "We can do that, Cande. Now that I have a job...I'll save up for this adventure. We'll call it our Special Night Together. And, it'll be just you and me, okay?"

"I'll save all the soft drink cans and we can recycle them. That should get us a couple of bucks."

"I can save them, too. I'm sure Jack will let me have the ones at work. It's a good thing that the people that work here are not hassling us for sitting here even though we finished our meal an hour ago. I like that."

"All right!" Cande shouted happily. "This will be our special place."

They talked until the bus arrived. They boarded it and arrived safely home where Beaver spent the rest of the evening reading magazines while Cande painted.

Six weeks later, Beaver and Cande found the restaurant closed for employee vacations. They decided to walk five blocks to the El Fénix Restaurant. As soon as they entered the restaurant, they realized how crowded the place was. Beaver fidgeted. He hated crowded places and wanted to leave, but Cande was hungry. Beaver glanced around. After a short wait, they were shown to a table and a waiter took their order. As Beaver surveyed his surroundings, he remembered that his mother had loved to come here, especially after being to a dance. As a young boy, he had gotten to tag along once or twice and he remembered the way her eyes lit up whenever they came to this particular restaurant. "Cande, do you like it here?"

"Yeah! I like those paintings on the wall."

A waiter came up to their table and said, "Beaver!"

Beaver glanced up and recognized Jay Orta. Jay had a tray full of empty dishes balanced on his shoulder. He wore a tuxedo-like short, tight-fitting black jacket with black pants. "Jay! Don't tell me you work here?"

"Hey, man, I gotta have money to go out!" Jay glanced at Cande. "Good to see you, kid. You were all of eight when I saw you last. You two guys still live in Ledbetter?"

Beaver nodded. "Sure. Where do you live?"

"The family moved to Oak Cliff a long time ago. I went to Sunset High, but I didn't finish. I've been working here about two years." He glanced nervously toward the kitchen. "Be back in a second." He hurried through the double swinging doors.

Beaver turned to Cande. "I went to school with that guy. It was a long time ago, but he obviously remembered me."

"I like his uniform."

"It's sharp. I'm sure he had to buy it just to work here."

Their food arrived and they ate heartily. Beaver was glad Cande was having a great time.

Jay stopped at the table on his way back to the kitchen. "Beaver, I've got an invitation to a Quinceañera tonight. Why don't you two come along?"

Beaver was taken by surprise. He hesitated, but seeing how interested Cande looked, he quickly decided. "Great, Jay. Where's it gonna be?"

"The Sheraton Hotel. Why don't you walk around the West End and come back at nine sharp. That's when I get off work."

Jay glanced toward the kitchen, then added, "I've got wheels. See you in the front of the restaurant at nine."

Cande glanced down at his shirt. "People dress sharply when they go to those dances, Beaver."

"Yeah, but hopefully it'll be dark when we get there and no one will notice us much."

He nodded. "Let's hope you're right, Beaver."

"Cande." Beaver leaned toward him. "What's the West End?"

A smile beamed from Cande's face. "That's right. You don't know about the West End." He laughed like a delighted child. "I get to take you to the West End! It's like a mall with lots of special shops, and it's only eight blocks away. I know it because Joe Columbus took a group of us guys there."

As it turned out, Beaver like the West End. He especially liked the carnival atmosphere filled with laughter and bright-eyed people. The shop windows were lined with bright pink and purple neon lights. Happy-go-lucky college kids filled the shops and restaurants. Beaver bought Cande a T-shirt, which Cande immediately put on. Beaver so enjoyed the atmosphere that he bought himself some freshly made chocolate candy. After that, they went out and sat on the plaza and listened to a concert. Beaver enjoyed just sitting there, watching all the people come and go. It was fun not knowing anyone and blending in with the crowd. No one took particular notice of them. They were just a couple of guys out on the town.

When Jay finally arrived, he looked great in a silk shirt and black dressy trousers. Spotting his friends, he motioned for them to join him.

"My car is in back!" Jay said. "And, I've got the invitation, too."

"Jay?" Cande asked, "Maybe, I shouldn't go. You can drop me off at home."

Jay and Beaver both said, "No way!" and laughed.

Jay added, "You look fine, kid... And anyway...this Quinceañera is a family affair. I know those people personally. So, don't worry. I'll get you home afterwards."

Cande frowned nervously then glanced at Beaver. Yes, Beaver had a right to have some fun. He'd been home more than a month and until now he hadn't been to a dance or even had a date. Cande agreed to accompany them.

CHAPTER SIX

Beaver was impressed by the thick pale-blue carpet that covered the hotel floors. He saw himself reflected in huge ornate mirrors and knew instantly that he didn't fit into this elaborate setting. His jeans were much too faded and his shirt was wrinkled. He glanced over at Cande and realized that Cande was feeling the same way. Jay examined his face in the mirrors and checked to make sure every hair on his head was in place. Beaver envied him. Jay looked as confident and sharp as the dandy that he was.

The elevator arrived. They got on and so did a couple dressed like they were going to a ball. The young woman looked like a princess to Beaver. She wore a red strapless dress that clung to her figure. Her hair was a deep red-brown and fell in waves down her back to her waist. The smell of her perfume, and of the cologne the young man wore, reminded Beaver that he didn't even own a drop of cologne. Beaver couldn't take his eyes off the young woman. To break his stare, Jay nudged him. Glancing at Jay to object, Beaver noticed that Jay's eyes never wavered from the girl's date, who had stepped forward to block Beaver's view.

"I'm cool!" Beaver whispered to Jay.

Cande shrank back to the rear of the elevator, and Jay stared at the floor numbers that flashed as the elevator moved to the top floor, hoping the date wouldn't say anything to him or Beaver.

Well, Beaver thought, he had an excuse to stare. It'd been a long time since he'd been so close to a pretty young woman, and he didn't feel he was being obnoxious. But it was obvious he'd put Jay and Cande on alert, so he stuck his hands into his pockets.

As the elevator moved upward, Beaver suddenly realized how much of the dating game and of his youth he'd missed during the last three years.

The couple exited the elevator and the trio followed them at a distance down a mirrored corridor to a ballroom.

"Jay?" Beaver asked nervously when he saw the security guard standing at the entrance of the ballroom next to a matronly woman who accepted invitations. "Are you sure we can get into the dance?"

Jay stopped walking and faced Beaver. "No sweat. I know these people personally." Jay moved directly behind the couple that had been on the elevator. Upon approaching the woman, Jay said, "Ah, *Señora* Cervantes, how beautiful you are tonight!" He smiled happily.

"Oh, Jay. How nice to see you. You are as handsome as ever." She accepted his invitation, never once taking her eyes off his.

Jay continued, "May I present two friends of mine. Francisco and Cande." Jay quickly drew Beaver closer to his side.

"*Mucho gusto,*" Ms. Cervantes said. "It's my pleasure, Francisco." She held her gloved hand to Beaver.

Beaver gently shook it. Her smile was genuine and he liked her. She had not even flinched at the sight of his old clothing. Ms. Cervantes looked like she was pampered by a doting husband and family. She then shook Cande's hand even though he was hesitant in giving it. "Welcome," she said, "to my granddaughter's Quinceañera. It is our pleasure to give her this fifteenth-birthday celebration."

"Thank you for inviting me," Jay said to her before he led Cande and Beaver into the ballroom.

A Texas-Mexican polka quickly vibrated off the floor up Beaver's toes and legs. The dance floor was crowded with couples whose eyes were filled with romance and excitement, and Beaver stood spellbound, watching them from a distance.

The round tables, which held perhaps a dozen people, were covered with white-linen tablecloths. Each had a cluster of pink and white balloons anchored to a basket of spring flowers. Beaver hadn't seen balloons in such a long time that the sight of them made him feel crazy, like a kid at his first birthday party.

Beaver and Cande tagged behind Jay as he made the rounds. He seemed to know everyone and shook hands with lots of people. Occasionally, he would introduce them to whomever he was speaking. Beaver let Jay be the hospitable one while Cande and he worked their way toward a suitable spot to stand. There, they listened to the music and watched the dancing couples as well as the young ladies that made their way back and forth to the ladies' powder room.

"Beaver, this is nice," Cande shouted over the noise.

Beaver nodded. "Do you know anyone?" he asked, spotting Jay's head pop up and down among the crowd.

"Just a couple of girls from school, but they're seniors."

"Well, point them out and introduce me!" Beaver asked.

Cande didn't answer because he'd turned to watch a group of kids standing nearby.

Beaver couldn't dance. It'd been ages since he'd tried, and the truth was that he just had never learned. He'd been to a couple of dances like this one, but he wasn't a guy to go zipping around the dance floor doing a polka with his arm clasped firmly around a young woman's waist, trying to show off with all those fancy steps. But, he did tap his foot to the rhythm. Cande, too, stood swaying slightly. Beaver could tell that he really liked the sound of the band.

"Hey, Beaver," Cande said as he leaned toward him, "I'm going to take a look at those monstrous speakers and watch the band."

Beaver nodded. "I'll be standing here." He watched his brother as he made his way toward the stage. Cande found a spot near the revolving lights that the band used as laser beams to shoot colored sparks onto the ceiling of the ballroom.

Beaver searched the crowd to find Jay, who was still on the dance floor, twisting left and right with that slight prancing pace of his while executing a Cha-Cha-Cha. Jay had completely forgotten about Beaver.

"Hey, guy. Can you buy me a beer?"

Beaver glanced to his left. There stood a young girl who seemed about fourteen, trying to act like she was twenty-one.

"How old are you?" he asked.

"I'm old enough," she answered, turning to the girl who stood next to her. The other girl, Beaver noticed, was taller, but seemed to be a year or so older.

"How old is old enough?" Beaver demanded, slightly annoyed.

"Sixteen," she blurted out quickly as another taller girl joined them.

"Beaver shook his head. "No way, girls. You both are too young to be drinking beer."

"Well, then," said the taller girl, "we'll buy you a beer and we'll take a sip of yours. Deal?"

Beaver stared angrily at her.

She quickly added, "My name is Lena."

"Nice to meet you, Lena, but I am not buying you a beer." Beaver quickly took her hand off his arm. He turned to the shorter girl, who had taken his other arm. She tried to smile seductively. Beaver laughed so loud that they were both startled.

The shorter young woman quickly said, "My name is Gloria." She moved slightly to the music. "We could really use a drink."

Beaver laughed at how grown up she was trying to act. "Well, Gloria, try a Coke. They're great! Or, maybe a ginger ale."

Suddenly, another girl dressed in a formal blue dress that matched those of the young women in the birthday girl's court in the Quinceañera appeared directly before Gloria. "Mom is looking for you! You'd better get over there now! You, too, Lena!" she fiercely commanded with an outstretched arm.

Beaver stood stunned. She was the prettiest young woman he'd ever seen. Her large black eyes blazed. Her long black hair kept falling forward just below her breasts in a mass of curls that coiled up and down like a car spring. He guessed her age to be eighteen, maybe, nineteen.

"You're both in deep trouble!" she continued, scolding her sister and friend and showing no embarrassment for doing so in public. "Mom has been ready to leave for the last twenty minutes!" She hesitated a moment to look at Beaver, wondering who he was. Their eyes locked and held for a moment.

"Who are you?" she asked as she turned from him to each of the young ladies, seeking an explanation.

"I'm Francisco," Beaver answered, and put out his hand to shake hers. "I guess Gloria must be your sister?"

She glanced down at his outstretched hand, then she gently took it. "Yes, Gloria is my sister."

"Good!" Beaver said, not knowing why he had said that.

"Good?" she quizzed, looking at him like she knew something had transpired between Gloria, Lena and him.

"Yeah, good..." Beaver glanced at Gloria who stood nervously tugging at his shirt sleeve. "Now, if you could get Gloria to her mother, I'd be glad to buy you a Coke, or anything you want," Beaver added softly.

Gloria gasped. Her hand released Beaver's arm and covered her mouth. Lena looked up at the ceiling as though she were swearing.

"Regina," Gloria replied angrily, "don't you have a guy waiting to dance with you?"

"No, I don't, but you two have Mom waiting to pinch your arm."

Lena and Gloria dropped Beaver's arms and quickly left.

As Regina turned to watch them leave, Beaver asked, "Regina...is that your name?"

"Yes," she answered, glancing at his hair. "Regina Barbosa."

The music Beaver heard in his ears was slow and mellow. "I would like to buy you a Coke. Will

you let me?" Beaver tried to sound as persuasive as
he could.

Regina looked confused for a moment, then
turned to watch Gloria and Lena as they disappeared into the crowd. Her curly hair brushed
against the skin of his arm and Beaver shivered,
feeling as if he'd been mortally wounded.

"I don't know," she said, hesitating. "I mean,
not now... I have to take Mom and the girls home.
But I'll be back. Maybe then," she added, looking
down at his faded jeans. She then looked deep into
his eyes, and Beaver almost sank to his knees.

"Okay," Beaver whispered in a choked voice.
"I'll wait. I'll look for you later."

"Fine," she answered as she turned and walked
away.

Beaver got very restless after Regina left. He
wanted to walk her to the car and go with her, even
if it meant taking her mother, Gloria and Lena
home. Hey, Beaver, he said to himself, you're crazy!
You've lost it. Instead of following his impulses, he
went and stood next to Cande and constantly
searched among the crowd for the return of a young
woman named Regina Barbosa.

CHAPTER SEVEN

Beaver spotted Regina as soon as she walked into the ballroom. It had seemed like hours since she'd left to take Gloria and the others home. From the distance, she looked beautiful. Beaver watched her from the corner of the ballroom. Two other guys talked to her. She smiled a lot depending on whom she spoke with, and accepted a Coke from one of the guys.

Beaver was anxious. He wanted to go up to Regina and shove those guys out of her way. What if she'd forgotten about his offer to buy her a Coke? Jay had said that she was a real nice girl and came from an educated family. Beaver suddenly felt inadequate. So what, he thought. He had his G.E.D., and that was a good start.

Jay had laughed when Beaver mentioned that he had met a girl named Regina. "Man," Jay had added, "her folks are teachers...and the hardest teachers in school! I remember all the guys dreaded their classes. Ms. Barbosa taught English and Spanish in middle school and Mr. Barbosa taught English and Math in high school. If you lived in the west side of town, you'd have to have one of them as a teacher. Beaver, I flunked Mr. Barbosa's class. I'll never forget that. So, even though Regina's good-looking, none of the guys will have anything to do with her. Like, what if she gets mad and cries to her old man and you just happen to have him for English. He'll make life real tough for you, that's for sure." Jay flexed his shoulders as if to shake that terrible thought. "Beaver, I can see the way you're looking at her. This is not a smart move."

"Jay, don't worry about me." Beaver moved slowly through the crowd of bodies toward her.

"Hey, Beaver, listen to me!" Jay yelled as he watched his friend zig-zag through the crowd.

Beaver didn't want to hear Jay. He didn't want to take his advise and miss his chance to get to know Regina. Who cared what her parents did for a living or what her sister looked like. Who cared about the English classes. Not Beaver. All he did know was that this young woman was like a giant magnet. Her beauty drew him to her and he couldn't resist. He walked toward her, letting her radiance reach out and envelop him.

Suddenly a pair of arms reached up to embrace him. "Beaver?" A girl hugged him tightly. "It's been so long." She kissed his cheek.

Beaver tore his eyes away from Regina for a moment to stare at the person acting like an obstacle in his path toward Regina. Margie Martínez smiled. She was teasing him with her winning smile.

"Margie!" Beaver immediately returned her hug.

"Beaver!" she said as she cupped her hands against the sides of his face. "It's really you."

"Margie, it's good to see you." Beaver pulled away from her. "You look great! Where's your husband?"

"At the bar as usual," she replied, embracing him once more. "Beaver, you've lost weight. Are you out for good?"

He nodded happily. "Yes! It's great! How are your kids?"

She held up three fingers. "There are now three beautiful little girls."

"Three!" Beaver replied in wonder. "One for each year that I've been gone."

She nodded. "Faith is two, Melissa is three, and Carmen isn't even a year old."

"You and Richard have three babies?"

She laughed, "It's been hard, but we're all right. I mean we still have a problem with his drinking, but everything else is great." She looked serious. "Did Cande tell you I was going over to your place to check on him while you were away?"

"No! He didn't!"

"He probably forgot," she quickly added as she pulled back her long glossy brown hair over her ear.

"I just got in town. Cande and I are still trying to catch up on three years that we lost."

"Good! We live in Irving now. We left West Dallas two years back."

Beaver put his arm over her shoulders and she wrapped hers around his waist. They walked off the dance floor and bumped into Regina who quickly glanced from Beaver to Margie and then immediately walked past them.

"Oh, darn," Beaver moaned.

"Who is she?" Margie asked curiously.

"A young woman...that's all," Beaver replied as he watched Regina take to the dance floor with some other guy.

"I can see! She's pretty. Well, come on, let's find Richard."

They moved toward the bar and Margie immediately spotted her husband leaning against the counter. "Richard!" she yelled over the noisy bar. "Look who I found."

Richard turned and grinned sheepishly. "Francisco! Glad to see you!" He held out his moist hand.

Beaver shook Richard's hand, trying not to stare at Richard's bloated face. Beaver knew that Richard and Margie had gotten married right after he was sent to prison. When he had heard the news, he had felt a great sense of loss. Margie and Beaver had been inseparable since they were toddlers, and there was a deep bond between them. Beaver could see that Richard was into drinking. His eyes were already glazed over and he was perspiring heavily. Not good, Beaver noted, glancing at Margie whose eyes had taken on a dark, hardened stare.

"Richard, it's been a long time," Beaver said, putting his hand in his pocket and not failing to notice that Richard glared back at Margie as if to warn her not to say a word about his drinking.

"Right, Francisco. It's been a long time." He turned his attention to a man standing beside him.

Beaver glanced at Margie, noticing her nostrils flare. She was angry, and for a second her face betrayed her unhappiness.

Cande suddenly joined them. "Margie!" he exclaimed happily.

Margie hugged Cande, then started scolding him. "I'm angry because you didn't tell Beaver that I visited you while he was in prison."

Cande hung his head a little. "I just didn't get around to it...that's all."

She smiled. "It's okay, Cande." She turned to Beaver. "Why don't the two of you come over for supper tomorrow evening about six?"

Cande's eyes lit up. "Sure, Margie! I love the way you cook!"

Margie was pleased. She clasped Beaver's arm tightly. "We'll have fun tomorrow. It'll be like old times."

Beaver glanced at Cande. He could see that his brother was really counting on going over, but Beaver felt it'd be best to stay away from Richard. He had detected a hint of jealousy in Richard's manner and that bothered him. He needed to get out of this sticky situation. "Margie, we have plans..." he added. A hand gently touched his shoulder. Beaver glanced back, thinking it was probably Richard ready to sock him in the jaw. He saw Margie's eyes narrow a bit, and he quickly reacted on finding Regina standing there.

"You promised me a Coke," she said softly. "Remember?"

Beaver glanced at Margie and Cande and saw the surprise on their faces. Margie was inspecting Regina up and down. Cande started to sway from one side to another as if he were real nervous. The words didn't seem to want to come out of Beaver's mouth as he moved to Regina's side and gently took her elbow. They moved to the bar where Beaver ordered two Cokes. Taking the Cokes, he found a dark spot in a nearby corner.

"Regina, I saw you when you got back from taking the family home, and I was going to you, but Margie suddenly caught me."

She took a sip of her Coke and smiled. "She likes you very much. I can tell that." Her eyes drifted to where Margie stood with Cande and Richard.

"Yes, but she's married to that guy at the bar."

He watched as Regina's eyes looked at Richard. Beaver wondered what she was thinking? Could it be that she was jealous of Margie? Could it be that Regina got angry because she saw Margie throw her arms around his neck and smother his cheek with a kiss? Not knowing what Regina was thinking, Beaver didn't say anything and took several sips from his Coke. He was nervous and noticed that each time he brought his Coke to his lips, his hand trembled slightly as if he hadn't eaten in a long time and the hunger pains were throwing his body into a frenzy. Before he realized it, he had finished his Coke and so had she.

Beaver took Regina's hand and urged her onto the dance floor. He faced her and looked into her eyes, all the time fearing he'd fall in love with her, a beautiful young woman who was educated, who came from a family of teachers. Never did it dawn on him that he didn't know how to dance, that other people stared at them, labeling them the mismatched couple of the night. All he cared about was that he was holding Regina in his arms as he moved to the slow rhythm of "Color My World." As Regina's black curls caressed his cheek, he felt like he was finally home. He was finally out of prison for good. That part of his life had never existed. He pulled her closer as the knot in his throat swelled and a tear fell from his eye. Thank you, Lady, he thought for this moment which he would never forget. He smiled when he felt Regina tighten her embrace and lightly caress the back of his neck. Beaver glanced at the huge clock that hung on the wall over the bar. It was exactly midnight as "Color My World" ended, and they drew slowly apart. He walked her back to the dark corner and they stood with hands clasped together. Regina didn't talk and neither did he.

Beaver thought of the time that Joe Columbus had discussed love with him. Beaver had been sixteen when Joe Columbus had closed the center and had turned to find him standing alone in the shadows.

"Beaver! You startled me, man! What's wrong? You're never here this late?" When Beaver did not speak, Joe Columbus knew he had a problem so he had continued, "It's a beautiful night, Beaver. The moon is full...it's a time for love and for life." He had put his arm over Beaver's shoulder. "Do you want to sit on the bleachers and discuss what's eating you up?"

They had sat in the dark, looking up at the moon and the north star. After a while Joe Columbus had continued, "In Indian territory up in Oklahoma, on a beautiful restless night like this when there was no woman to comfort you, a group of guys would get together and drive up to this high peak, a mountain, really, with a flat top." He had chuckled as if the memory brought him immense pleasure. "We'd build a fire and sit around it, talking about love and how the young ladies changed our lives. We'd talk about what we liked about our young ladies. The old wise woman of the tribe said that a man never marries the woman he truly loves. I don't believe that. Things just happen to change the course of life." He was silent for a long time, staring up at the moon with such intensity that Beaver had looked away, wondering if he'd ever be as smart as Joe Columbus.

"Who is your true love, Beaver?"

Beaver had sat forward. "See, I've got this problem with Margie. I've known her since we were little kids. Now, I suddenly get these feelings that if I let go and lose control, I could really hurt her. I gotta stay away from her, but I don't know how much longer I can push her away." Beaver had taken off his bandana and wiped his face. "What am I going to do?"

"I didn't know it was like that between you two. You'd never know it in public. You both hide your feelings well."

"Yeah, but when we're alone it's a different story."

Joe Columbus laughed. "I know that feeling, and I also know what you can do, Beaver. Tell her that you're going to finish school and that she must finish as well before you can think of a permanent relationship. It might work."

Beaver glanced up at the moon. "I'll try that, but I don't know that it'll work."

Joe Columbus had stood and said, "Let's go to Wimpy's for a hamburger and Coke."

"Let's go!"

Beaver smiled at the memory of that moment he'd shared with Joe Columbus, but as he glanced up, he saw Margie at the bar sitting next to Richard, whispering into his ear. Whatever she'd said to Richard did not seem to please him. "You're special," Beaver whispered, feeling an ache for Margie and the situation she'd have to live with for the rest of her life.

"Did you say something?" Regina asked, turning to face him.

Beaver took a lock of her hair and gently pulled it. "I said you are special."

She smiled and pulled him out to the dance floor once again.

As the magic of the night progressed, he realized that they didn't say much to each other. It was as if words were not necessary. Beaver saw the rose color of her skin and the little beauty marks that were sprinkled like stars upon her face. Her lips were curved and full, shaped much like a valentine. A blue-velvet ribbon hung over her right ear, holding back her swirling black curls. The rich smell of perfume held him spellbound.

He vaguely remembered Cande coming up to him to say that Margie and Richard were going home and that he wanted to hitch a ride with them. Beaver remembered nodding as Cande turned to join Margie and Richard. Beaver had turned his attention back to Regina who blushed, but never took her eyes off his.

They danced many times until the lights were turned on and the band announced that the dance was over.

Jay appeared from among the thinning crowd and said, "I'm ready to leave, Beaver. I gotta work the lunch crowd tomorrow."

Regina quickly said, "Give me a minute to get my flowers, Francisco."

Beaver let go of her hand and watched as she hurried to the table where her flowers were set.

"Jay, I think I'm in love," Beaver blurted out.

Jay grunted, "Sure, Beaver. I know how that is. Come on, let's hit the road. I'll drop you two guys off, then head out to Oak Cliff. Where is Cande?" he asked, turning from side to side looking for Cande.

"Cande?" Beaver suddenly remembered. "He went home with Richard and Margie."

Jay looked startled, then he paled slightly. "Richard is a drunk, man. How could you let your brother go home with him?"

Beaver looked flushed. "Hey, I've been gone. How was I supposed to know for a fact that Richard was a lush. Besides, Margie is with him." Jay started walking away. "Hey, hold it. I have to get Regina's phone number. I'll meet you outside...at the car, Jay."

Jay turned back. "Hurry, man. I'm tired."

Beaver moved across the dance floor to where Regina was saying goodbye to some other girl-friends. He took her elbow and gently pulled her away from them. "I'm leaving. Can I walk you to your car?"

"Sure, Francisco."

She waved goodbye to another girl, and Beaver escorted her out the nearest door, down the elevator, and into the parking lot.

"Are you going home alone?" he asked, concerned that no one else would accompany her."

"Yes," she laughed. "I only live ten blocks from here! I'll be okay."

"Are you sure?" he inquired, taking the keys from her hand and opening the door to her small blue sedan. "I mean, I'll be worried."

She shook her head. "I'll be fine, Francisco."

"Can I have your phone number?" Beaver asked, looking out over the parked cars for Jay's automobile. "I'd like to call you sometime," he added as he looked down to his feet.

She smiled, then reached into her car for a pen and paper. "This is my number. But, I work after school and it's late when I get home. So call me after nine at night."

"I'll call." Beaver gently squeezed her hand and she got inside the car. He stood watching until she drove off.

Suddenly Jay drove up next to him. "Let's go. I've been waiting forever!"

Beaver jumped into the car. "Jay, this is the best night I've ever had in my entire life."

"Hey, man. You're just feeling grand because this girl gave you all her attention. You'll get over it. Besides, there are plenty of chicks out there. You've been in prison too long to let a single girl throw you crazy!"

Beaver felt that Jay was trying to dampen his spirits, and he didn't say much as they made their way up the two-lane highway.

Suddenly Jay had to pull to a quick stop. Cars were lined up bumper to bumper as far as Jay's eye could see.

CHAPTER EIGHT

Jay leaned out of the car window hoping to see what was holding up traffic. "Darn!" he cursed. "It must be a wreck. Cars are lined up for miles! I can't see a thing!" He cut the engine and groaned. "Ah, man! It'll be another hour before this mess clears up and traffic starts to move."

"I guess we don't have a choice but to sit tight and wait," Beaver added, suddenly hearing the sirens of an ambulance in front of the multitude of cars. He glanced around the area then added, "There's no other way out of here." Beaver looked over at the car parked next to them. He didn't recognize the couple, but Jay did, and before Beaver knew it Jay had gotten out of the car to talk to them. Beaver opened his door as well. He went around the hood of the car, then walked over to the middle of the lane to glance in the direction of the wreck.

A guy ran up to the car next to them and yelled excitedly. "There's been a real bad wreck! Three ambulances so far! They say it's some people who were at the Quinceañera."

"Who are they?" Jay questioned.

The guy shook his head, "I don't know." He hurried to the car behind Jay's, relaying the information as he progressed onward.

Beaver's stomach felt queezy and his knees felt like buckling under him. An urge to run toward the scene of the wreck overtook him. Before Jay could turn toward him, Beaver was racing between the lines of cars heading for the site of the wreck.

"Beaver!" Jay yelled. "Come back! What's up?"

Lady, Beaver prayed, don't let it be Cande. He pushed people out of his way so he could run forward, zig-zagging between cars and couples. The sinking feeling he felt in the pit of his stomach intensified and the Lady on his back seemed unusually heavy. He was so scared that chills ran up and down his back. His heart beat as if it would burst, but he ran onward without stopping. Perspiration ran freely down his face. Never mind that people stared at him. His instincts told him that he needed to find Cande. His mind told him to be prepared for the worst, but his heart begged for all this to be nothing more than his imagination...like just another bad dream. As he hurriedly glanced around the crowd near the wreckage, he could not see his brother. Perhaps Cande had made it safely home. He scolded himself. How could he have let Cande leave the dance, knowing Richard had been drinking heavily. My Lady, he pleaded, you should have warned me! You should have opened my eyes so that I could see the danger!

Beaver stopped running. Before him, the red, flaring lights of the ambulances and squad cars warned him of the worst. Paramedics worked frantically to help the injured. Nearby lay the body of a man covered in yellow plastic. It was a man, Beaver noticed, because men's black dress shoes protruded out from the yellow plastic. Cande had tennis shoes. Beaver knew that for sure.

Several cops and medical personnel were huddled over another injured person. Beaver hurried to them, but he could not get a look at the person who lay on his back. A cop finally rose slowly. Beaver moved forward to speak to him, then stopped, wanting to throw up as he recognized the person lying down. He saw blood covering Richard's face and oozing out of his mouth. Beaver screamed and tried to get to Richard as a policeman forcibly held him back.

"Stop!" the cop ordered unceremoniously.

Beaver didn't know if Richard was unconscious or dead. He stood a moment trying to collect his wits. No, he reasoned, if Richard were dead, that yellow plastic would be covering him.

"Cande!" Beaver yelled, wildly searching for his brother. He ran up to another cop. "I'm looking for my brother. He's wearing tennis shoes, white ones! Let me look over there." He pointed to the wrecked car where firemen and policemen were struggling to free the door. Suddenly realizing that Cande might be trapped inside, he shoved past the cop and ran to the opposite side of the car. The front end crushed like an accordion, all neatly folded and tucked in two.

Beaver stood away from the door hesitantly, fearful of what he might find. The men on the opposite side of the car moved frantically. They spoke in hushed tones as they worked diligently with a torch. They had draped a heavy canvas over one window to prevent sparks from harming the person still trapped inside. In the back seat of the car sat one medic, and another knelt near the door, equally busy with needles, bandages and bottles. No one took notice of Beaver as he slowly moved to the opposite side of the car. Then he bent inside the shattered window and clung to the door as he felt himself go weak.

Beaver recognized Margie's dress. Her arm, cut and bloody, hung limply upon the seat. Her face was partially covered to prevent the sparks from burning it. Her eyes, which in the past were so merry and gay, were closed. A peaceful semblance illuminated her face, but from her lips flowed a slow trickle of blood.

"Margie?" Beaver whispered as he limply clung to the door of the car. "Margie?" Somehow from the hushed whispers of the men working on her, he knew that she was still alive. He willed her to be alive. Beaver had heard that the last sense to leave a dying person was hearing. "Margie," he whispered lovingly.

Beaver reached inside the window and took her hand in his. The medic looked at him curiously, then nodded gently when he realized that Beaver was holding Margie's hand. The medic continued to monitor her pulse. "Margie?" Beaver whispered. "Sweet Margie!"

Tears stung his eyes, but he did not feel them. The pain in his heart was of such magnitude that he found it hard to breathe.

He heard himself crying as if he were a lost child separated from his mother. "Margie? Don't leave now, Margie," he repeatedly whispered. He felt a slight squeeze from her hand and looked at her face. Yes, there was a smile. A smile for Beaver, her favorite person in the whole wide world. He knew she'd heard him because she squeezed his hand once more, this time ever so slightly.

"Oh, God, Margie, what do we do now?" he asked helplessly, then gently kissed the palm of her limp hand.

After a moment, the paramedic slumped back into the seat and wearily wiped his forehead. He looked at Beaver sadly. His blue eyes were moist and filled with regret. "She's gone," he said in such a soft, tragic tone that Beaver understood that the medic had hoped that he could save her. The medic waited a few seconds, then in a firmer, louder voice he said to the other men working near the door, "I lost her."

If there was shame in crying before other grown men, Beaver did not know it. He only felt a searing hurt inside his heart as the sudden image of a Queen of Hearts card flashed before him, then shattered into a million pieces as if a bullet had been shot right through it. He knew how much Margie had cared for him and that she had also considered Cande as part of her family. Beaver would miss her more than anyone else in the whole world. The men moved away from the car, but Beaver stayed holding her hand, not wanting to let go. He simply couldn't let go of Margie. She was special. She was his childhood friend. She was the girl who pointblank told him, "I know you didn't hold up that Jack-in-the-Box, Beaver. You're not like that." And she was the young woman at his trial reaching over and saying, "I'll be with you forever."

The medic eased Beaver away from the car. He guided him over to the side of the road. "Are you okay, buddy?"

Beaver looked away as he wiped his eyes with his bandana.

The paramedic spoke earnestly. "The engine crushed her legs from the hips down. I only hope the morphine I gave her eased her pain. She was conscious in the beginning, but she went out fast. I tried my best to help her. I'm sorry."

Beaver shook his head as a way of telling him that he understood. They stood together in silence for a time before Beaver realized he still needed to find Cande. "Was there another boy in the car?" he asked. "A kid, about sixteen."

The man's eyes blinked rapidly. "Yes, he went in the first ambulance. Two boys, as a matter of fact."

"My brother wore tennis shoes and jeans," Beaver added quickly.

The paramedic nodded. "You'd better get to the County Hospital."

"Thanks, mister," Beaver said as he hurried to find Jay.

Jay was pacing furiously around his car, kicking the tires every now and then as he cursed under his breath.

"Jay!" Beaver screamed. "We need to get to the County Hospital! Cande's there!" He pulled open the car door as Jay hurried to the driver's side.

"Man, you're crazy! Running off like that. People thought you'd lost your brains... What hospital?"

"Richard had a wreck!" He hesitated and swallowed. Then he stated, "Margie just died...and Cande's in the hospital!" He grabbed Jay by the arm and shoved him into the seat. "Now get us out of this traffic jam even if you have to drive over the other cars!"

Jay sat stunned a moment, repeating Beaver's words. "Margie, dead?"

"Yes. The medic said she was crushed from the hips down. It was a bad scene, man. All I know is that Cande's hurt. Let's go!"

Jay managed to get out of the tight squeeze between two cars and drove rapidly down a steep grassy incline without batting an eye. Beaver was scared the car would roll over and kill them, but Jay moved onward fearlessly.

CHAPTER NINE

Jay and Beaver arrived at the hospital and hurried up to the information desk. The clerk said that she didn't see Cande Torres' name among those recently admitted. Beaver quickly explained about the wreck and that there had been another boy in the ambulance as well. "The paramedics," Beaver emphasized, "told us that the ambulance was coming to this hospital."

"Well," she added hesitantly, "I'll call down to emergency. He might be too recent for me to have any information on the case." She quickly dialed four numbers, then smiled when she had the answer she wanted. "You need to go immediately to the emergency room and see the intake clerk," she told them.

"Thanks," Beaver mumbled as he headed in the direction of the elevators.

From the directory, Beaver learned that the emergency room was downstairs. They took the elevator down and immediately stepped into a well-lighted area crowded with what seemed like hundreds of idle people milling around. Beaver spotted the intake clerks, but gasped when he saw the lines of people waiting to see her ahead of him. "We'll never find Cande!" He stood a few restless moments, then suddenly burst out of line and rushed to the clerk. "I need to find my brother, Miss! He's been in a wreck and is here somewhere!"

"You have to wait your turn!" she insisted.

Beaver pleaded with her. "Please, Miss! Check this out for me." Beaver could tell from the way the corner of her thin lips fell that the woman couldn't care less if Cande was alive or dead. She continued working on her computer terminal. Beaver immediately slammed his fist down on the counter, causing her to lean away. "Look!" he said more calmly. "He's my only brother. Our mother is dead! He has no one but me."

The clerk rose and disappeared behind a door that led to the rear of the counter.

"You got a lot of nerve busting the line!" a woman said directly behind him.

Beaver turned back to her and answered, "This is an emergency, lady."

"So! What do you think I'm here for?" she retaliated, stepping closer to Beaver as if she were going to shove him back.

Beaver looked angrily at the woman, who instantly closed her mouth. She stepped away from him just as the clerk returned, followed by a security officer.

"We have two unidentified boys who recently arrived. Their ages are about fifteen. This is Officer Lorenzo." She pointed to the man directly behind her. "He will take you to where they are to determine if one is your brother. And, young man, mind your manners in there!"

Beaver reached over the counter and gently squeezed her hand. "Thanks, lovely lady," he whispered while the security guard in the brown, starched uniform came around the counter and motioned for Beaver to follow him.

The woman in line angrily elbowed her way to the counter, determined that she should be waited on promptly.

Officer Lorenzo took them up an elevator, which stopped on the 9th floor. Two doctors entered and the elevator proceeded to the 10th floor, where the doors rumbled open and everyone got out. Beaver and Jay followed Officer Lorenzo down a long corridor. They went through some double doors and entered a circular area which contained the operational nucleus of the emergency ward. Officer Lorenzo pointed out a satellite area used as a waiting room. Jay and Beaver went over and took a chair.

Beaver marveled at the sight before him. Nurses and doctors dressed in light-blue scrub outfits rushed to patients behind draped areas. Stainless steel computerized machines ticked loudly, doing blood work-ups and whatever else was needed to facilitate the diagnosis of the doctor. Everyone talked in hushed, controlled voices. Beaver suddenly realized how narrow his education had been and how little he knew about other aspects of life outside of his immediate experience. These people were highly educated. They were trained beyond his comprehension and they talked a strange dialect which was fascinating to hear. They seemed to talk like characters in a science-fiction movie, and they understood each other perfectly. They were almost God-like, Beaver thought to himself as he waited patiently. He turned to make a comment to Jay, but found him leaning back against the wall with his eyes closed.

Beaver knew Jay was tired, but so was he, and Beaver's anxiety level was killing him. He rose and paced back and forth in the small confined area. Through the glass partition he could see Officer Lorenzo talking to a doctor, who quickly motioned to a section and then accompanied the officer over to a bed. They stood talking a moment, then Officer Lorenzo turned and went to Beaver.

"Over this way," Officer Lorenzo said to Beaver, quickly glancing back at Jay who was still leaning heavily against the wall and snoring lightly.

Beaver followed the security guard and stood as the officer pulled back the drape so Beaver could see the person on the bed. Beaver shook his head. The boy before him was not Cande.

Officer Lorenzo moved to the next bed, and this time Beaver immediately recognized Cande as he lay with his head bandaged. One of his legs was supported by a traction device. "Jesus!" Beaver moaned as he moved to his brother's side. "Cande?" he said softly, but then immediately realized that Cande was unconscious.

"Is he your brother?" Officer Lorenzo asked as he took out his pad and pen then shot one question after another at Beaver.

Beaver answered as he tenderly held Cande's cold hand. The officer soon stopped the questions and went to speak with another person. "My Lady," Beaver prayed silently, "Cande never hurt anyone. Help him." Beaver suddenly became aware of a doctor standing next to him.

The doctor was an older man with a shiny bald head. "You could use some sleep, young man," he said to Beaver. "This young boy here is making some Z's!" The doctor chuckled to himself more than to Beaver as he continued. "He has a broken leg, a broken hip, and a slight head concussion. His left wrist is definitely broken. Where are his parents?"

"Dead!" Beaver said, ticked off by the doctor's attitude which he did not appreciate at this most serious time. He saw a confused look break across the doctor's face. He quickly added, "Mom is dead."

"And his father?"

Beaver shrugged. "Might as well be dead."

The doctor muttered that he was sorry to hear that and moved away. It was some time before Beaver noticed that the doctor talked in hushed tones to the officer in a nearby corner, but he turned his attention back to Cande, whose eyes were bruised and swollen. Beaver knew that his breathing was extremely shallow, but thanked his Lady for sparing Cande's life. He was also happy that it was Cande's left hand that was broken, not his right, which meant he could continue to paint.

The guard came over to Beaver and announced that he had to go downstairs to fill out some papers. Beaver reluctantly followed, but he noticed that the doctor kept staring at him oddly. Hadn't Jay scolded him last night about needing to correct his manner of approaching people? Beaver got frustrated so easily in crisis situations. He stopped a moment and smiled. Then, in a softer-than-usual voice, he said to the doctor, "Thanks, Doc, for taking care of my brother."

Beaver entered the small glass waiting area and shook Jay awake. They followed the guard down numerous halls as Beaver explained Cande's condition to Jay. When they arrived at an office in a remote section of the hospital, Jay looked confused, then glanced over to Beaver who sat and waited. Something, Beaver felt, was coming down and he knew Jay sensed it as much as he did. "I don't like the smell of this, Jay," he added nervously.

Jay grew still. "Neither do I."

"Just be cool, Jay," Beaver warned as an officer approached them and asked that Jay follow him. Jay rose and glanced at Beaver, not knowing what to say, then turned to accompany the officer to another room.

Another officer approached Beaver. "Come with me, son."

"I don't understand!" Beaver argued. "I haven't done a thing!"

"We know that, son, so calm down." He took Beaver to another office and closed the door, then motioned to a chair. "Have a seat. I'm Officer Hampton." He went around the desk and flopped into a swivel chair. "Now, tell me what you did today."

Beaver told him about going out to eat with Cande, of meeting Jay and ending up at the dance. He even told him about Regina. After he'd explained everything, he asked, "What have I done that's so wrong?"

"I'll answer that question in just a moment. Wait here." He opened the door and called out to Officer Lorenzo. "Stay here until I return."

Beaver watched Officer Lorenzo make a couple of phone calls. He decided that what he'd done must not be so bad, because Officer Lorenzo was quite lax in his attention toward Beaver.

Within a short time, Officer Hamilton returned with Jay. Motioning for Jay to sit, he stated flatly to the nervous young men, "Well, your stories are the same." He cleared his throat then looked directly at Jay and said, "You can go home."

"What about Beaver?" Jay asked.

Officer Hamilton looked at Beaver. "Francisco." He looked down at some papers quickly. "The doctor says that your brother has had some bad injuries for some time. He's filed a complaint of child abuse, stating that Cande Torres has been a victim of physical abuse for quite a while." He studied Beaver.

Beaver was stunned. He couldn't even speak. He remembered that Ms. Chavarría had said that his father had been beating Cande, but he had no idea that it was for a long time. Beaver sat forward and nervously rubbed his hand over his forehead. "And you think I abused him," he said quietly between clinched teeth. "I swear that I didn't touch Cande. I love Cande. He's my brother. He's all the family I got!" His voice was raised to such a high pitch that Beaver found himself suddenly standing. Then he paced back and forth. He was losing his cool as he turned to look at Jay, who looked quite frightened.

"Francisco," Officer Hamilton said, "we know you were released from prison six weeks ago. We've checked with your probation officer, who is on her way here now. We know you're not the person we're looking for, so calm down." He pointed to the chair, clearly indicating that Beaver was to sit immediately. Then he turned to Jay. "Why don't you leave now? Ms. Rodríguez is on her way here and she can give your buddy a lift home."

Jay looked at Beaver for some kind of approval. Then Beaver nodded.

"Okay, I'll split now. Be cool!" He nodded slightly at Beaver and left.

Officer Hamilton and Officer Lorenzo stayed with Beaver in the small enclosed office located in the basement of the giant hospital. Beaver didn't feel threatened or scared, but he felt like killing his father for hurting Cande. After he had calmed down considerably, he found himself wondering if the hospital morgue was nearby. That scared him even more than the thought of killing his father.

A social worker named Ms. Turner from Dallas County arrived. She requested to see Cande and to speak with the doctor. Ms. Turner was pleasant and very soft spoken. From the way she dressed, she too must have been at a party. A beeper was clipped to the strap of her handbag. A child-abuse social worker, she glanced at Beaver with dark eyes filled with concern.

Officer Lorenzo quickly offered to take Ms. Turner upstairs to see Cande. Officer Hamilton poured Beaver a cup of coffee and asked him some more questions. He kept coming back to questions about Cande's father, and he asked questions that Beaver couldn't answer. Beaver knew that the officer suspected his father. Beaver, himself, wanted to blame the whole thing on his old man.

For Beaver to place the blame on his father was easy. He knew his father for the angry person that he was. Beaver wanted sweet revenge for the countless times his father had kicked him out of the house in the middle of the night, forcing him to spend the night curled up on a lawn chair in Ms. Chavarría's yard, listening to his mother cry and his father scream right back at her. He knew that his father was very irrational, almost blood-thirsty. Yes, he knew his father would be the ideal candidate to commit the abuse, but all Beaver had to go on was Ms. Chavarría's word.

By now, Beaver was really tired. It was four in the morning. He rubbed his hand wearily over his face. Officer Hamilton was talking on the telephone at a nearby desk. His back was turned, so Beaver figured that he was pretty much off the hook.

Suddenly, Ms. Rodríguez burst into the office, startling everyone in the process. She looked like they'd just pulled her out of a warm bed. Her eyes still had that lazy, sandman look, making her seem less harsh. She wore a slightly wrinkled jogging suit and her hair was flying in all directions. Later, Beaver would find out that her hair was like that because she drove a Volkswagen convertible and she had not bothered to put the top up. Ms. Rodríguez glanced at Beaver, then asked, "You all right, Francisco?"

By the time Beaver had nodded an affirmation, she'd turned to Officer Hamilton and they were speaking in hushed tones. After a while, she turned to Beaver and said, "Come on, Francisco. We're going upstairs to see Cande."

Beaver was up in an instant, but he was not fast enough to catch Ms. Rodríguez, who was already out the office door and walking down the hall toward the elevators. "Wait up, Rodríguez!" Beaver shouted. "Man, you'd think Cande was your bother instead of mine!"

She turned to look at him at the elevator door and watched him as he caught up. "Francisco, have you had contact with your father?"

"No! Look, this is how it is. Every Friday and Saturday night, Cande and I go out to get away from the house, in case he drops by. Ms. Chavarría, our neighbor, said he'd been hitting on Cande, but I didn't know whether to believe her. Hey! I've been gone three years and Cande never said a word about this to me. I swear this is the truth, Ms. Rodríguez!"

The elevator doors finally opened and they entered. "Okay, I believe you, but this is going to be a problem."

"In what way?" Beaver asked, curious at her statement. Ms. Rodríguez was closed-mouth until the elevator arrived at the proper floor. "Let's check on Cande," she said softly. At the door to the recovery room, she hesitated as if she was afraid to go in.

Funny, Beaver thought, maybe she's afraid of hospitals. Maybe he'd discovered her weak spot. He'd store that piece of information in his memory bank.

"Okay," Ms. Rodríguez said twice before she finally flipped her purse strap over her shoulder and led the way through the doors.

It had been more than two hours since Beaver had seen Cande.

He was still unconscious or sleeping, as the doctor said, but his vital signs were good, according to the doctor, who talked to Ms. Rodríguez for a long time, then gently put his hand on Beaver's shoulder. "He's resting. I think it'll be tomorrow before he comes around. Go home and get some rest yourself."

Beaver looked over at Ms. Rodríguez, who was speaking to Ms. Turner. He gave Cande's hand a gentle squeeze and said softly, "I'll be back tomorrow, little brother."

Ms. Rodríguez came to the bedside and said, "The doctor says he'll be fine." She turned to glance at Beaver. "Let's get you home."

Beaver didn't want to leave Cande. It tore him up to leave his little brother, who looked more defenseless than ever. He adjusted the blanket that covered him, then reluctantly followed Ms. Rodríguez to her Volkswagen.

The cool morning air and the slight mist that lingered before daylight was enough to push the tiredness away from him. "Ms. Rodríguez," he said, "I like your little bug."

She didn't answer, but she did smile.

When they arrived at his house, she slowed down and passed it, then went around the block and passed it again. "I believe it's safe," she added.

"I could have told you that no one was there," Beaver replied, getting out and letting the door slam shut.

"Hold up, Francisco. I'm going inside with you."

Beaver waved his hand in objection. "It's not necessary, Ms. Rodríguez."

"Yes, it is, Francisco." She gripped her purse in an unusual manner and followed him. "You got a key?" she whispered.

"Hell no!" he snapped angrily. "There's no lock or bolt on the door, so we don't need a key."

"Not smart, considering the circumstances, Francisco. I'll get someone over to fix it."

"I give up!" Beaver muttered scornfully as he walked inside the house and flicked on the lights. "See, not a soul here, Ms. Rodríguez."

"Not much here at all, Francisco," she said as she walked around the room and into the kitchen, then moved cautiously to the back door. She tiptoed down the hallway to the bedroom. Beaver tried not to laugh out loud and anger her. She looked so unlike the professional woman that had sat before him in her office. Of course, he had to remind himself, it was now five in the morning and all the circumstances were extraordinary.

She got to Cande's room, hesitated at the doorway, then slowly entered. He decided that he'd better follow her. He found her at the closet. She was on her knees, studying two of Cande's paintings. "You do these?" she asked.

"Cande painted those. He's going to be an artist."

"He's got talent, that's for sure," she added. "Tell him that I want to buy the red roses." She proceeded to check the bathroom. "Okay, Francisco. I'll be here around noon to take you to the hospital."

"Ms. Rodríguez, I can take the bus," he pleaded, weary of her presence.

"You can take the bus home after your visit." She left the house and hurried to her car. She was off in a minute, but she circled the block twice.

He turned away from the door so tired that he didn't care if someone jumped from the shadows and beat up on him.

The next morning Beaver had barely showered and shaved when he heard Ms. Rodríguez honking. He pulled on his jeans, grabbed his shirt and bandana, then raced to the car.

She was dressed in a red suit and had her hair pinned up. She looked rested.

Beaver smiled as she greeted him with a singing hello. She was obviously in a good mood, but Beaver didn't feel all that great. His head ached, he was still tired, and he hadn't had time for breakfast.

After arriving at the hospital, she said, "I'm going downstairs. You can go up to see Cande. I'll meet you there."

Beaver agreed, and they parted at the elevators. Cande had been moved to a ward with four other patients. When Beaver got there, Cande faintly smiled. Beaver could tell from the sparkle in his eyes that he was glad to see him.

"Beaver," Cande said, "I want to go home."

Beaver nodded. "As soon as they let you, pal. I'll get you home...you can count on that. Okay?" He carefully pulled a lock of Cande's hair.

"Okay," he responded, "but, Beaver, I feel like shit!"

"Then sleep, little brother. It's the best thing for you. You can't go anywhere right now."

The corner of Cande's lips turned upward in a slight smile as he closed his eyes. Beaver stood next to him, wondering how he was going to tend to him once he did get him home. His leg was broken and Beaver was sure Cande's insides felt like mashed potatoes. He knew he had to work. Maybe Ms. Chavarría could help him. Beaver would ask her as soon as he got home. He was sure she'd do it. After all, Cande was like a son to her.

He stood staring down at his brother, his little shadow. They had roamed the streets of West Dallas together as bonded friends, blood relatives for life. Suddenly Beaver chuckled to himself. The streets and alleys of West Dallas would outlive both of them, and that was the reality of their lives. Beaver suddenly felt sick in the pit of his stomach. This little, underweight bag of bones was all he had in his life, and he didn't want anything to separate them again.

Ms. Rodríguez stood next to him. He didn't look at her, but he'd heard her pull the drape back. "Have you talked to the doctor?" she asked.

"No. Cande was awake when I got here. He said he wanted to go home."

He looked at her and saw that she'd paled.

"What's the matter?" he asked.

"Home?" she said hesitantly. "Well...to be honest, he won't be going home for a long time, Francisco. I thought you realized that."

Beaver stared at her. "What do you mean?" he asked.

She looked flustered and quickly clasped her hands. Then she lifted some hair out of her face. "Early this morning, the police picked up your father. He's in jail. It's like this... Your mother is dead, Cande is a juvenile, that means he's under age and he has no available guardian. He'll be placed in a foster home. In simple terms, Francisco, it's like Cande belongs to the state now, and not to you."

"Ms. Rodríguez!" Beaver screamed as he grabbed her by the shoulders. "You can't do this! He's got me. I'm here now!"

She moved away from him and shook her head. "You're on probation, Francisco. Have you forgotten? You're not eligible for guardianship. It's just not possible." She walked to the foot of the bed. "Hey, I'm sorry, but my responsibility is to you, not to Cande."

"Do something, Ms.Rodríguez! Do anything! Just get him home!"

"Let's go outside where we can talk."

Beaver took Cande's hand as he angrily retorted, "How can this be happening. We were all right! For six weeks we'd survived and were happy. Ms. Rodríguez, I was fixing up the house, and I got a job. I'm supposed to take care of him, not some dumb people he doesn't even know!"

"Francisco, keep your voice down and come with me!"

Beaver reluctantly followed her outside the hospital to a small garden where they sat on a concrete bench. "Francisco, it's not like he'll be gone away forever. You can visit him. He'll get regular meals. Someone will be with him all the time. It's not so bad," she reassured him.

Beaver hung his head. "Yeah, like prison wasn't so bad either and I got regular meals there, too. Hell, I cooked those meals! I don't like it, Ms. Rodríguez! Cande is a gentle guy. Most of those kids are rough. I know, because they all ended up in prison with me. I'm twenty-one, Ms. Rodríguez. Why can't I take care of him?"

She sighed heavily and paced back and forth. "It can't be done, Francisco. Not while you're on probation. Maybe, in a year, with your best behavior... who knows? Tell you what. Let's wait and in six months or a year from now, I'll give custody a shot. For right now, I'll talk to Ms. Turner and recommend Hope State Home. It's an okay place. I was raised there myself and I turned out pretty good, and so did a lot of my friends." She laughed nervously, then added, "I don't tell many clients that, so keep it to yourself."

Beaver stared at her, speechless. "You... at Hope State? Impossible!"

She nodded, and with a quivering voice replied, "Yes, I'm a product of Hope State Home. I was five when I got to Hope. I was abandoned, so it was the only place where they could place me. The people at Hope State were good to me. They were good to all the group—if you followed the rules. Everyone has rules, Francisco... even Presidents have rules, you

know that. It's just a matter of following the rules...
of knowing your limits."

"Yeah, but you...at Hope State? Look at you. I
mean...you're a probation officer and you dress like
you're somebody."

"It took me many years to be this somebody you
see, and I hope that means I look like a professional. It was hard being without a family... I don't
remember much, but anyway, that part of my life is
over. It's out of the way, so to speak."

Beaver saw no tears spilling over her face.
She'd resigned herself to her fate long ago.

"Prison is in my past, too, but that doesn't help
Cande much. Ms. Rodríguez, I know you can think
of something. You have to try. There's no one else to
help me now. This is a tough jam. I mean, I got
plans for Cande. He's going to finish school and he's
going to be a famous artist." Beaver pleaded without pause.

"So, his plans are on hold for a little while. It
doesn't mean he can't accomplish his goal. And
Beaver, maybe, you should worry about your future
and your goals. If you're true to your word, you'll be
there for him...and that's more than I had. Look,
he's going to recover. That'll take six weeks, maybe
more. His schoolwork can be taken to him and he
can finish this school year. In the meantime, we
have problems with your father that we've got to
deal with immediately."

"That man was a problem for my mother, Ms. Rodríguez. I don't want to see the bastard!" Beaver turned and ran down the stone path.

"Francisco, you have to deal with this!" she screamed.

Beaver turned to face her and yelled, "Wrong! The police have to deal with him. He's out of my life! I won't have anything to do with him except kill him, if I ever get my hands on him!" He ran into the hospital, leaving her standing with her hand on her forehead like she had a migraine.

Beaver was more worried than ever. Cande at Hope State! Impossible! He'd run. Yes, Beaver would run away with Cande, but Cande was too sick to go anywhere. What could he do?

Beaver arrived at Cande's bedside and took his hand once more. It was ice cold and he started to cry silently. "Damn this world!" he cursed. It seemed the prison walls were closing in on him again and he hated the squeeze.

CHAPTER TEN

Beaver stayed at Cande's bedside all morning. Cande finally woke up and smiled at his older brother, then muttered that he hurt all over. Beaver gently brushed Cande's hair back, knowing that he needed to tell him about Hope State, but he lost his nerve and skirted the subject. Soon Cande dozed off. Beaver walked down the corridor and onto the elevator. As the elevator moved downward, a depression seized Beaver. If his mother were alive, he could talk to her about his feelings of emptiness. He needed direction. He needed someone to tell him what to do, as they had done in prison. He thought of Jack at the tire shop. They had become good friends. He knew Jack would listen to him, but he might just as easily understand as not understand, depending on the nature of the situation. He could also talk to Joe Columbus. Yes, Beaver would try to find the time to see him. The elevator opened on the first floor of the hospital and he immediately saw a phone. Quickly he dialed Regina's number, and she answered.

"Regina," Beaver said, "this is Francisco."

"Hi!" she said softly. "How are you?"

"Regina, listen. I'd like to speak to you...about something that's happened. Could we meet in an hour or so?"

"I guess so, but where?"

He smiled for the first time that day. "Could we meet at the tennis courts at Sunset High School? I'll take the bus to meet you there."

"That's not too far from my house," she responded. "I'll tell Mom that Gloria and I are going to play tennis. Mom never lets me go anywhere without Gloria. You know that, don't you?"

"Oh, great!" he moaned, but he wanted to see her and if that meant Gloria's hanging around, then he'd have to tolerate it. "Okay, bring Gloria," he added. "No, problem. I'll see you at four this afternoon."

It was a few minutes past four when Regina drove up to the tennis courts. Beaver watched from under a large shade tree as she slowly opened the car door and stepped out. She wore jeans and a white oxford shirt that fell open to her knees. Underneath the oxford shirt, she wore a sleeveless baby-blue T-shirt. She surveyed the area quickly, spotted Beaver, then pushed the car door closed and hurried toward him.

"Regina!" he shouted as he waved to her. "I expected Gloria to bounce out of the car. Where is she?" he asked as he walked slowly to meet her.

Regina laughed. "Gloria is home watching videos. Mom didn't force her on me like she usually does."

Beaver took her hand and they walked slowly to a nearby shade tree. Holding her hand gave him instant encouragement.

"Beaver," she said, softly turning his face toward her. "You look like you've been through a tornado. What's been happening?"

Beaver was surprised. "Yeah, I must look pretty bad. I need to talk to someone or I'll go crazy."

She shifted nervously. "Are you in trouble?"

"No, but trouble surrounds me like a dark cloud. Sometimes, I can't see through that cloud. It's like I can't find my way for the darkness suffocating me. People talk about their future, but I don't have a future...no tomorrow, no nothing." He sat on a bench and sighed.

"Talk like that scares me. You sound like you're ready to commit suicide or something." She sat next to him and watched the sun reflect off the vacant tennis courts. "You can talk to me."

When Beaver told her about the events that had occurred the night before, he noticed that she did not move away from him, but sat staring off into the distance as if in deep thought.

"Unbelievable!" she commented. "This morning Tila called me and told me about this bad wreck she'd heard about, but I didn't think much about it." She hesitated then asked, "Is there anything I can do?"

Beaver shook his head. "Not really. I know I'm no angel, Regina. I never was and I never promised to be. I did a lot of wrong things in my life, but I was never intentionally bad."

She remained silent, listening to him, not daring to say a word lest it break into his thoughts.

Beaver continued. "Now, my father is bad. It seems like he was born bad. Sometimes I believe that he can't help himself. It's his bad ways and that's all there is to it."

Regina sighed heavily after he'd finished telling her the story of his life, then added, "Why don't we go to the Bear Pit for hamburgers and fries? My treat!" She stood and reached for his hand.

Beaver didn't object. He was hungry. They didn't say a word as she drove to the Bear Pit and found a spot that was a little away from the other parked cars.

After they'd ordered, she started talking about her life, her family, and how much she liked school. "I'm going to be a teacher, Francisco. I've always wanted to be a kindergarten teacher. My folks are teachers. I'd bet you'd like my folks. It's hard to get them out to dances and parties. They'd rather be home reading, but occasionally Mom will go with us to weddings and parties."

Beaver responded gloomily. "They wouldn't like me if they really knew me."

"You never know about them."

He smiled and added, "Sure, but everybody knows what an ex-con is and I doubt they'd accept me as a suitable companion for you."

"You can't judge for them. A lot of people judge other people, but my parents have never been judgmental."

Beaver shook his head. "No, I suspect they'd judge me real quick! Even though I've got my

G.E.D., bad blood runs through my veins and I'm plagued by bad luck."

"I think that's silly. Blood is blood. It's all in your mind. Think positively, Francisco. That's the key. My mother always tells me to find a way out of a bad situation. Solve those problems that stand in the way of your goal. I dare you to do that, Beaver. I double dare you."

Beaver reached out and gently tugged one of her curls. "Maybe," he mused, "I just might take up your dare."

"My Mom has never failed me. We talk about things, you know."

Beaver let go of her hair and said, "Then I'm glad she's your mother. Take care of her. You never know when she'll be gone, then you'll miss her so much it'll burn your soul."

"Burn your soul?" She glanced at him seriously. "I wonder if Margie burned your soul with scars so deep you can't forget her?"

Beaver smiled and looked away as an image of Margie flashed through his mind. The thought saddened him. Maybe if they'd stayed close, Margie would be alive today. It's useless to think such thoughts, he decided with a slight shrug of his shoulder.

He didn't let her drive him home because he didn't want her to see that his house was a dump. Instead, she drove him to a place where he could catch a bus directly home. "I'll call you," he said.

She smiled. "Sure, Francisco."

"Great!" he added as he shut the car door.

"Francisco?" she asked softly. "I wish you'd let me drive you home. It's getting dark."

Beaver shook his head. "No, Regina. I'll be in touch." He watched her disappear into traffic. She was such a simple young woman, he thought to himself. She had a glow of health about her. Even though she was an honor student, she didn't flaunt it, and she didn't put him down because of his lack of education or his not being the big football hero.

Beaver rushed to work and found Jack waiting for him in his office at the tire shop. Jack threw him a set of heavy keys. "Open up the place," he said, "and let's hope for a slow day."

"Jack," Beaver said, "my little brother is in the hospital. He was in a bad wreck Saturday night. As soon as I leave work today, I need to go to the hospital."

Jack slowly pulled his leg down from the top of the desk and looked at Beaver. "I see," he said seriously. "What's happened to him?"

Beaver filled him in on all the details. Jack sat still a long time. "Watch those social workers," he commented. "They pull a lot of strings. Some of them do good and others do more bad then good. I had to deal with plenty of them while my wife was ill. Tell you what, Beaver, I'll let you go at four this afternoon so you can catch an early bus to see Cande. In the meantime, let's open up and get this day started."

Beaver nodded then smiled, glad that Jack understood the severity of the situation. He hurried to open the place up.

All morning Beaver worked hard so as to forget his troubles. Then, he prepared lunch for Jack and himself. He fixed soft tacos filled with fried chicken strips, lettuce, sour cream and guacamole.

Around three, Jack went over to Garza's Bakery. When he returned, he called Beaver over and handed him a brown paper bag. "This is for Cande."

Beaver glanced into the sack. There were a couple of car magazines and a box of cookies. "That's nice, Jack. Thanks." Beaver said in a soft voice.

"The cookies are from Garza. He's also heard about the accident." Jack paused, then asked, "I guess you'll be going to the funeral, too?"

Beaver felt as if Jack had thrown cold water over him. "I don't know, Jack. I've been so wrapped up in Cande and his problems that I forgot about Margie...and her funeral."

"Garza said it was at ten tomorrow morning at the Laredo Church down the street. Go ahead and go. I'll handle things here until you get back."

Beaver nodded and silently turned back to his work even though he didn't feel like doing a thing. He knew that he should have gone to see Richard and the girls, but right now all he could think about was Cande and the problems that overwhelmed him.

Margie's service had already started when Beaver entered the church and quickly slipped into a pew at the rear. Beaver noted the white roses that covered the white casket like a warm blanket. He knew she'd like that. He concentrated on the tranquil glow of light emanating from the stained-glass window as the priest continued the Mass in Spanish.

Beaver tried to put himself in a soothing trance by staring at the flickering candle lights, but all he could think of was how worried Margie would be about Cande. "Margie," Beaver vowed in a reverent whisper, "I'll look in on your daughters as you cared for Cande while I was holed up in that stinking prison. That's my promise to you."

Beaver didn't go to the cemetery. Instead, he walked over to the little grotto which surrounded the statue of the Virgin of Fatima and the statues of the three children to whom she appeared in the Cova da Iria in Fatima, Portugal. He sat on the cool concrete bench in front of the statue and saw that the face of the Virgin was sad and seemed to embrace his sorrow. Beaver glanced at the faces of the children. Rapture and happiness radiated from them. The sculptured hedges that surrounded the site seemed to protect him during his moment of vulnerability and sorrow, and he was glad of it, so much so that he felt like lying at the feet of the Virgin and sleeping. The leaves of the tall shade tree that stood directly behind the Lady's statue rustled and calmed his turbulent spirit. There, Beaver whispered his private "Adiós" to Margie.

Beaver felt despondent and melancholy about the situation Margie's daughters were in. He had gone over to see them the day following the funeral. The girls hadn't even realized that their mother was dead and that they would never see her again. They were much too young and innocent. Their grandmother, Margie's mother, was taking care of them. She was quick to tell Beaver that Richard had taken off right after the funeral and no one had heard from him since. They were hers now and she would raise them the best she could. From the tone of her voice, Beaver knew that this woman was capable of killing Richard if he showed his face at her house.

"Would it be okay if I drop in to visit the girls?" Beaver asked. "I'm sure when Cande gets well, he'd like to visit as well." He glanced up at the old woman.

"Oh! Please come. Come over anytime." She gazed at the girls playing under the shade tree. "They don't understand. They're babies."

Beaver nodded. "I haven't told Cande that Margie is dead. I have to do that soon."

The woman turned her attention to Beaver. "Yes, you must tell him soon."

Beaver rose. "If there's anything you need, let me know. You can find me at the tire shop."

"Bless you, son," she said as Beaver opened the front gate to leave.

A week had gone by since Cande was hospitalized, and Beaver had spent most of his free time at his brother's side. He now held Cande's hand tightly.

Ms. Rodríguez suddenly appeared at Beaver's side. "Cande looks a lot better. There's more color in his cheeks," she said. "How are you, Francisco?" she asked matter of factly.

"How'd you know I was here?" Beaver questioned, disturbed by her intrusion. He guessed he'd never get used to her showing up at any given moment without warning. It was like she could sense where he was.

"Well, this is your free day and you're not at home, so I figured you'd be here. Where else would you be?"

"With a girlfriend," Beaver said smartly, intending to upset her.

"A girl already? You work fast, Francisco."

"What do you want, Ms. Rodríguez?" Beaver asked harshly.

"I came to let you know that you can forget the foster home. I was able to get Cande into Hope State. I thought you'd be pleased."

Beaver remained silent until she said, "You have visiting privileges and... after he's well, you might get to take him home one weekend per month. Isn't that great?"

Beaver stared at her, then asked, "How long does he have to stay there?"

She pushed the hair back from her face and looked over at Cande. "For a while...maybe...a long while. Until the end of the summer...perhaps."

Beaver sat down in the chair and rubbed his forehead. "Are you talking about a year, Ms. Rodríguez?"

She nodded, "Yes... Maybe longer...unless you have a relative with a spotless reputation, who has a job, who works regularly, who can offer the kind of care Cande needs, and who wants to be declared his guardian. Then we can get him out in a month or so."

Beaver shook his head wearily. "There's no one except some people in Mexico, but I don't even know their names."

"No uncle or aunt here in the States?"

"No."

"Well...I've set up a tour with the Hope State people on Saturday. It'll be good to see the place again." She smiled. "Francisco," she said seriously, "right now, it's the only way. The place is not so bad. Take my word for it." She grabbed her purse and said, "At least he won't be abused again." She turned to leave. "Jack at the tire shop said it'd be okay if you left Saturday for a couple of hours."

"Thanks," Beaver responded. "Jack's a good guy."

Hope State was in East Dallas. Ms. Rodríguez had explained that it would be easy to get to, even by bus, and Beaver found out that she was right. The red-brick main building sat in the middle of several acres of land. It was surrounded by smaller buildings that had ivy growing on the walls.

Beaver met the director, Ms. Howard, and several dorm parents who lived in the cottages. Ms. Howard was a prim, older lady in her late sixties. She was reassuring, and Beaver saw that she obviously knew Ms. Rodríguez from way back. From their occasional laughs and hugs, Beaver noted that Ms. Howard was very proud of Ms. Rodríguez. He visited the classrooms and heard the director explain how some children were candidates for adoption and others had parents who were in crisis and were temporarily housed there until their parental situations improved. The older children were bused to nearby schools. Beaver visited the cafeteria and saw the spacious kitchen. The gym was also large and well-equipped. There was even a swimming pool. Cande would like the place, he thought to himself.

Beaver asked about Cande's schooling. "He can't go to school with a broken leg. I don't want him to get behind in his schoolwork."

Ms. Howard nodded as if she understood, and Beaver could tell from the gleam in her eyes that she liked the question. "You are right. He'll be tutored until he is well enough to go to school. Then, he can be bused to school."

They went to see the dorm. Cande was to share a room with a young man named Eric who seemed to be about ten. "How long have you been here?" Beaver asked Eric as he looked over the room, which was large and much nicer than any Cande had ever lived in.

"A long time. Ever since I was a baby. Are you going to be my roommate?" Eric asked in an earnest voice.

Beaver immediately turned to him and laughed. "No, I'm kinda old to do that, but my younger brother will be here."

"Oh, good!" Eric got off the bed. "He's lucky. He's got a brother. When is he coming?"

"He's in the hospital right now, but he'll be here soon. I'll be visiting often. Maybe, I can see you, too."

"Yeah!" Eric shrieked happily.

Beaver shook Eric's hand. "Great, little man." He turned to leave the room to join Ms. Howard and Ms. Rodríguez who were waiting downstairs.

As Ms. Rodríguez drove Beaver back home, he thought about the situation. Hope State wasn't so bad. Beaver liked Eric, so he knew Cande would like the boy as well. Hope State seemed like a college, not the confined prison ground that Beaver had originally thought it might be. Maybe Cande would even be happy there.

"What do you think?" Ms. Rodríguez asked, interrupting his thoughts.

"I'll let Cande decide," Beaver replied quickly.

She smiled as if she knew she'd won this round. "I know you feel that this isn't the best place for Cande, but with time you'll see that it is."

CHAPTER ELEVEN

The next day, Beaver worked unusually late. He had no desire to return home and not find Cande waiting for him. He took his time clearing away tools and making sure everything was in order before he quit for the day.

Jack noticed that Beaver had been extremely quiet. He hadn't muttered three words while he was preparing lunch and only answered Jack's questions out of politeness. Jack watched Beaver, sensing the boy's detachment to his everyday duties, but he did not comment, feeling that it just wasn't the right time to say anything. Finally, as Beaver washed his hands, Jack could not resist speaking to him. "Beaver, you seem depressed...like my wife used to be when she got in one of her moods. I know you've got a lot on your mind, but I want you to promise me that tonight...well...you'll keep your nose clean and stay out of trouble." He gave Beaver's shoulder a tight squeeze to let him know that he wasn't angry, but worried. "That boy in the hospital needs you now." He reached into his pocket and pulled out some money, then paid Beaver for a week's work.

Beaver looked into the man's eyes and smiled. "Yeah, it's been a tough week and I'm tired, Jack. Wish I could sit somewhere and mellow out with a cold drink and forget that I ever existed."

Jack chuckled. "I used to do that in the garage just to get away from my wife, who considered the house her territory and the garage my place. Yep, I'd sit there with an ice chest by my side, glance at my garden and read. Take a tip from an old man, get a good book or magazine and sit in your living room and read. That'll keep you out of worldly trouble, if you know what I mean. I know that Ms. Rodríguez is checking you out pretty often." He dried his hands on a towel and ran a comb through his hair. "If you get real out of sorts, just come on over to my house. I'll be there... Ain't got no place else to go."

Beaver smiled. "I'll remember, Jack. I just might show up."

Beaver closed the lock of the chain-link gates and waved to Jack as he drove off in his truck. Walking slowly home, Beaver found himself smiling as he thought about Jack. He knew the old man was lonely. Heck, Beaver thought, he, too, was lonely.

He debated on calling Regina, but then he'd have to walk back to the shop to use the phone. It was too hot to do that and, besides, he felt extremely dirty. He decided to take Jack's advice and stay home. He'd grab something to eat, then lay in bed and read a magazine.

He found himself smiling as he thought about Jack. When the old greaser had found out about Cande and his artistic talent, Jack had gone out and bought Cande an expensive easel and various tubes of paint, then had taken them to the hospital.

Beaver had been touched. "Jack," Beaver had commented, "you've done enough. I don't know what to say anymore, except thanks." But in his heart, he wished he and Cande had had a father like Jack, who was so giving and understanding.

"Don't thank me," Jack had insisted, snickering like an old dog snoring in his sleep. "Never mind, son. Listen, I'm an old fart. My wife is gone. My kids are in California. They hate Texas weather. But, I've got you, Beaver. To be honest, you're making the business more money than it's ever produced before, so I've decided to raise your salary to eight dollars per hour." He reached out and gently shook Beaver's shoulder. "I mean to say...that you make life a little easier, so why shouldn't I also make life for you and Cande a little easier."

Beaver knew that Jack went to visit Cande on Sunday afternoons. On his first visit, Cande had immediately recognized him and had smiled. "Thanks for the paints and that great easel," he had said cheerfully while shaking Jack's hand.

Cande was recuperating slowly. He didn't sleep as much anymore, but he was still on pain pills. He was anxious to get out of the hospital, Beaver believed, just to get into the paints that Jack had given him.

Beaver reached the house, took a quick bath, then eased himself into the nicest shirt he owned. He would catch a late bus to visit Cande. After all, he'd spent the morning with Ms. Rodríguez at Hope State and then completed the workday. As he waited for the bus he thought about Regina. He'd really like to go to the movies with her tonight, but it was best if he went instead to visit Cande.

As soon as Beaver arrived at the hospital, he glanced at the clock on the wall. The nurse's station was busy as usual. Beaver went into the ward and found Cande watching television. He smiled on seeing his big brother. "Hey, Beaver! You look great! Are you going out tonight?"

Beaver smiled. "No, I cleaned up just to see you."

"Sure! Like I'm going to believe that."

Beaver looked over at his leg. "Doing better, brother?"

Cande's face looked sad. "The pain never seems to go away. I hate the pills they give me, but they do help the throbbing in my leg. Beaver, I just want to go home. When did the doctor say I could get out of here?"

"Cande," Beaver moved closer to him and gently straightened the blankets, "I've gotta tell you something." Beaver stopped speaking and took several deep breaths. "This is real hard for me to say, but I gotta tell you." Beaver looked at his brother's dark eyes. "You see, you aren't coming directly home. You need some special care. You'll be going to Hope State Home to stay for a while, or at least until you're better." He closed his eyes, not wishing to see the expression on Cande's face.

"What are you talking about?" Cande exploded angrily.

Beaver put his hand on Cande's to calm him. "You need attention that I can't give you. After you're better, you can come home." The expression on Cande's face gave Beaver the chills. "Ms. Rodríguez is going to help me get custody of you. That means I'll be your guardian. I went with her to visit Hope State. It's nice, Cande. Nicer than anything we've ever had. I even met your future roommate, a boy named Eric."

Cande stared at Beaver with an incredulous look, then blurted out, "I like my room and I want to go home, not to Hope State. You think I don't know about that place?"

Beaver shook his head, refusing to hear anymore. "No, you don't know!" Beaver quickly moved to the foot of the bed and soothingly ran his hand through Cande's hair. "I don't mean to be hard on you, but it's like this, Cande. Dad's not an option, and Mom is dead and, unfortunately for you and me, I won't be allowed to be your guardian until I prove myself worthy. Remember, I have a prison record, Cande, and that's not a good thing. Ms. Rodríguez explained things to me. So did Ms. Turner." Beaver looked directly into his younger brother's eyes. "Listen, it's only until you get well and I can straighten up things on my end. Then, you can come home and we'll be a true family."

Cande didn't say anything for a long time, but his chin quivered and his eyes were moist. Beaver knew that Cande was acting out of fear.

"Beaver," Cande said softly, "I'll go to Hope State, but only because you served time for something stupid that Mingo and I did, and now I'll repay you by going to Hope State. It's like that, isn't it? I mean, we have a deal?"

Beaver smiled, "Yeah, we have a deal, but the only difference is that I'll visit you every weekend and call every day. Now that Jack gave me a raise, I'm putting in a telephone just so we can call each other every day." Beaver squeezed his hand. "It'll be okay, Cande. I promise you."

"Did you like Hope State, Beaver?"

Beaver nodded. "Yeah, it's like a college. You know, Ms. Rodríguez grew up there. I liked it, Cande. And, I know you will, too."

Cande looked away from his older brother and studied the cast on his own leg.

"Cande, remember, I'll be there. All you have to do is be happy and become a famous artist. I'll do the rest."

Cande looked away from Beaver and remained silent for a long while.

"What's the matter, Cande?" Beaver asked. "I know things look rather bad now, but everything is going to be all right."

Cande quickly turned to Beaver. "Nothing will ever be the same. You see, Ms. Turner brought a lawyer to see me yesterday. They want me to testify in court that Papa beat me." He stared at the ceiling a moment before saying, "What should I do? I'm all mixed up, Beaver."

Beaver sat on a nearby chair and sighed. "You have to tell the truth, Cande. That's about the only thing to do. In the meantime, I'm going to ask Ms. Rodríguez about it."

"Beaver, what if I'm in court and I start crying or something embarrassing like that?"

"I'd take the stand if I could, Cande. You know I would, but I was in prison when all this was happening. I promise you that I'll help you get through this, and if you want to cry, then go ahead. No one will say a thing. Besides, Mom would appreciate you telling the truth. When this is over, you and I can get on with our lives. Hey, guess what?"

"What?" Cande sobbed, trying to keep himself under control.

"While you're away at Hope State, I'm going to enroll in junior college. The college downtown has a great cooking school. I've already called. It's a two-year program. I think I can do it, Cande."

"You a chef!" laughed Cande amid the tears. "That's really funny, Beaver!"

"Hey, I've got a new plan. I'm going to be a world famous chef! I'll work in a real fancy restaurant someday...just like you're going to be a world famous artist. Maybe, I'll get to that fancy cooking school in Paris."

"Beaver, you might make it to Paris, Texas," he added as his older brother playfully pounded on his good shoulder, "and work in some small restaurant."

"No, man...I mean Paris, France, and since you'll be a famous artist, I might even take you with me."

"Hey, you bet your last dollar that you're not going to Paris, France without me!"

"I'm glad you said that, Cande. I'd be awfully lonely without you."

That night as Beaver tossed in his bed, he thought about the possibility of really going to culinary school. Yep, it was a goal. A plan for a new life. Both he and Cande were getting new starts in life. The cooking school in Paris, now that would really be something to work toward. Dreams, he thought. Why not dream really big? After all, there was no one to stop him except his own imagination.

CHAPTER TWELVE

As the weeks passed, Jack became Beaver's companion and true friend. First, he helped Beaver get his house into shape, as together they painted the outside of the house. Then Jack called a friend and the trio replaced the sheet rock inside the small-frame two-bedroom house, but not before they added a big picture window in Cande's room, so that the young man could eventually paint by natural light. Beaver decorated the kitchen. He trashed the old yellow kitchen table, adding a large bar which gave him more work space. With two bar stools, this space would then serve as the eating area. He even made room on the bar to put the small television. It soon turned out to be a kitchen in which any chef would be pleased to work. Ms. Chavarría assisted by sewing curtains and keeping a close watch over the house while Beaver was in school two nights a week.

Jack also pulled Beaver out of his many depressed moods while Cande was still in the hospital. He would make Beaver laugh with stories of his youth. Often, he'd buy a new gadget for his redecorated kitchen, and would never say no to an invitation to a late supper.

Beaver, on the other hand, thought Jack hung around his house because of Ms. Chavarría's frequent visits. There's always hope for a new life,

Beaver thought as he watched the old couple from afar, never daring to ask Jack what they talked about.

Clearly, Jack was now his adopted father and there would be no replacing him.

Sometimes Jack would laugh at Beaver as they worked in the heat without their shirts. "Hey, kid. You know that Lady on your back? Well, she always comes alive when you move your arms."

Beaver would stop what he was doing and glance menacingly over at the man, warning him in a playful way, "Be good, Jack."

There were times when Joe Columbus would come over late at night and they would sit on the porch watching the cars drive by and other people just taking walks in the neighborhood. They'd talk about work, life and tough times, and would have a good time together. Joe Columbus made him laugh many times.

But the day finally arrived that Beaver had been dreading. It was time to move Cande from the hospital ward to the dorm at Hope State. To support his friend, Jack had given Beaver the day off so he could assist Ms. Turner and Ms. Rodríguez with the move. The previous night Beaver had washed Cande's better clothes, then neatly folded them and carefully placed them in a large plastic bag.

As he waited for Ms. Rodríguez, Beaver paced the living room floor. As soon as he heard her honk her car horn, he grabbed the bag and hurried out to meet her.

"Hi, there," she said with a wave of her hand. "Ready for the big day?" She glanced at Beaver as he arranged the bag in the back seat.

"Ready, Ms. Rodríguez," he answered.

"Nervous or not?"

Beaver stared at her for a moment then laughed, "You're kidding, right? Like I've served time, have you forgotten? It's like nothing makes me nervous anymore."

"Is that the truth?" she questioned. "I'll bet seeing your father at the trial next week will make you nervous. We need to talk about that, Beaver."

Beaver refused to talk to her and concentrated instead on looking at the houses that they passed on the way to the hospital. Besides, she was right. His old man did scare him, but he wasn't about to let Ms. Rodríguez know just how shaky he was getting.

"Hopefully, you won't have to take the stand, since you were gone during the abuse. At least, that's what I'm banking on. I'll do everything to keep you off the stand, but I can't guarantee it."

When they arrived at the ward, they found Cande sitting up in a wheelchair, his leg extended in a cast. Hearing Cande's voice cheered Beaver just as his younger brother's presence had spurred him onward when they had to hustle for food many years ago.

"Hey, Beaver, come over here!" Cande shouted.

Beaver moved to his brother's side. "Ready, Cande? The nurses tell me you're history here, man." He took off his bandana and wrapped it around Cande's head. "Time for you to move on."

"Yes," added Ms. Rodríguez as she turned the wheelchair and moved it slowly toward the bed. "The nurse will be here in a second. Let me check your closet, okay?"

Sitting on the bed facing Cande, Beaver noticed that Cande's eyes had gown sullen. "You okay, kid?"

Cande nodded. "Still wish I was going home, Beaver," he finally sighed.

Beaver nodded. "So do I, little brother, so do I." Then he continued, "I'm going to ask Ms. Rodríguez if she'll stop by the house so I can show you all the repairs Jack and I have completed. Let's keep our fingers crossed that she'll agree. I've got something I want to show you, something Jack and I are real proud of, even though he cursed up a storm while completing it."

Cande's eyes danced. He loved nothing better than surprises. "Yeah, and I want to take one of my paintings and hang it over my bed at Hope State. It'll remind me of home".

Beaver solemnly smiled. "I promise you, I'll get you out of Hope State as soon as I can."

A nurse and a male orderly entered the room. The orderly quickly glanced in the closet and in the bathroom while the nurse started wheeling Cande toward the door. "Time for you to go home, young man," she said gaily. Ms. Rodríguez and Beaver glanced at each other and followed her.

Ms. Rodríguez agreed to stop at the house after letting Beaver know that handling Cande and the wheelchair would be his task.

When they arrived at the house, Cande eagerly said, "I can hop, if Beaver will let me lean against him."

"You can always lean on me, brother." He took hold of Cande's arm and braced it around his shoulders. Ms. Rodríguez watched as the young men hobbled down the unleveled walk, up the porch and into the house. Beaver immediately took Cande to the kitchen. Cande suddenly tightened his hold on Beaver and his other hand moved to cover his eyes. He then slowly uncovered them and said, "Mom would love it, Beaver, especially the roses on the wallpaper." Then holding Cande steady, Beaver pushed open the door to Cande's room. "Wow! This window is...just what I need. Oh, man, it's great!" Cande tried to hobble inside without Beaver's assistance, but immediately lost his balance. Nonetheless, he glowed. "Tell Jack that it's great. I love it!"

Beaver chuckled. "Jack wanted to put in vertical blinds that pull away to the side, but I talked him into waiting until you come home so you could decide what, if anything, you wanted."

Cande smiled. "Leave it without anything for the time being. I like it like it is. I can see all of Mom's roses out back. It'll be wonderful, Beaver."

"It was Jack's idea."

"It's the best present I've ever had, except for that easel," he quickly added. "This whole place looks great. It's almost like new. You must have been working real hard."

Ms. Rodríguez stood patiently at the door. "We've got to go, guys. It's almost three in the afternoon," she reminded them.

Cande turned to her, and for a moment Beaver thought he'd say that he really didn't want to go, but Cande only nodded. Then, he requested of Ms. Rodríguez, "Would you please get the painting of the Aztec warrior out of my closet?"

"Sure," she said. She got on her knees to sort through the paintings in the closet. Her heart ached for the two brothers who only wanted to be together. She was too much of a realist, she figured, but the possibility of Beaver getting custody of Cande was almost impossible. From her social work experience, she knew that they would not be together until the youngest turned eighteen and Beaver was at least twenty-five. This must be the painting he wants, she thought. She studied the warrior a moment, then buried her face in her hands to hide the tears in her eyes and to allow the brothers a moment together to bid each other goodbye. She knew that she had to work hard to get the brothers together one way or another, and with God's help she would do it.

Beaver noticed that Cande seemed delighted to meet Eric. But, he slowly surveyed the room as Beaver eased him into his bed. Their eyes met and

Beaver said to his brother, "Just pretend you're on vacation. That's how I made it through those years in prison. You can do this, little brother, I know you can. I'll be here on the nights I don't have to go to school."

Because of the knot in his throat, Cande only nodded while Beaver continued. "Look, it's almost five o'clock and Ms. Rodríguez has to get back to her office. She's going to give me a ride home today, but I tell you what, I'll call to check on you from the phone booth at Sundown Grocery around eight. I'm sure they'll let me talk to you, since it's your first night here." He ran his hand through Cande's hair then slowly moved to the door.

"Beaver," Cande said, pulling himself up straighter in bed. "I'll miss you. I really will."

Beaver chuckled. "I know you will, kid. Just paint and you'll be fine."

"I'll paint something special for your kitchen wall."

Beaver smiled. Then he glanced back at Cande, who now looked very scared and sad. As he opened the door, Beaver waved to Cande. "Call you later, brother. See you, too, Eric," he added as he closed the door and moved down the stairs to join Ms. Rodríguez.

CHAPTER THIRTEEN

Ms. Rodríguez picked Beaver up on the morning of his father's trial. Afraid that the whole process would bring back some painful memories of his own trial, Beaver had not wanted to attend. But he went, knowing that Cande needed him.

Ms. Rodríguez and Beaver were both proud of how well Cande was doing at Hope State, and, for once, both were in agreement that Hope State had turned out to be the best place for Cande until Beaver could get custody of his brother.

As they drove downtown, Ms. Rodríguez said, "The summer is over, Beaver. You've kept your nose clean. I've got to say that I had my doubts about you in the beginning. I know that Cande and Jack have played a major part in your turn-around."

Beaver glanced at her. "Ms. Rodríguez, you've been wrong. I was a good guy all along. You judged me a bad guy because I had served time. But, you're right, Jack and Cande are the most important people in my life."

"Okay, you win. You are a good guy and it's really refreshing to know a good guy. In my line of work, they are few and far between."

Beaver saw his father for the first time in many years as he was brought into the courtroom. He had aged tremendously during the last four years. His skin, dark and weather-beaten, made him look even older. His back was hunched and he looked thin. As Beaver's eyes moved from the top of his father's head to his toes, he knew that he would never be afraid of him again. But, when he glanced sideways at Cande, Beaver could tell that his brother was in great fear of his father.

Beaver reached over to take Cande's hand. He squeezed it tightly and noticed that Cande kept licking his dry lips. Cande's eyes darkened and narrowed as he watched his father. Beaver leaned over to him and whispered, "Do this for Mamá. Just tell the truth and it'll soon be over."

Cande looked as if he had relapsed into a trance.

Beaver gently shook him. "You don't have to be afraid anymore."

Cande finally tore his eyes away from his father and nodded that he understood what Beaver was saying, but that did not stop his body from trembling. He constantly glanced at Ms. Turner, seeking reassurance. Ms. Turner frequently nodded her head, trying to let Cande know that everything would be fine.

Then Cande's name was called to take the stand. He rose slowly then moved toward the witness stand. He turned to face his father. The color drained from Cande's face as their eyes locked on one another. He grabbed hold of the wooden banister to steady himself, then his eyes quickly darted toward Beaver, who nodded, urging him to get hold of himself.

Beaver knew that Cande was frightened. He thought of his mother, wishing she were present to give Cande support.

"Please state your name and age," the attorney asked.

Cande answered clearly, "Cande Torres."

"Give me the names of your father and mother."

All through the questioning, Cande sat as close to the microphone as possible. He never looked directly at his father. His focus was on the attorney and Ms. Turner.

"He always beat my mother," he stated. "He slapped her across the face lots of times." And in a much lower voice he added, "I saw him punch her in the stomach. She couldn't eat for days afterward because of the pain." Cande hung his head and began to weep.

Seeing Cande so helpless upset Beaver. He quickly rose to his feet in an effort to assist his brother, but Ms. Rodríguez took his arm and gently pulled him back into the seat.

"Tell us about the times your father beat you," the attorney asked.

Cande studied his hands for a long time. Finally and with much hesitation, he described the times that his father beat him, including the time he lost consciousness.

"Why do you think he beat you?" the attorney asked.

Cande shrugged. "I guess because I look like Mamá... That's the only reason I could figure out. I swear I never talked back to him. Once he'd start hitting me, he'd keep hitting me." He paused, then quietly added, "He'd hurt me real bad."

Ms. Chavarría took the stand as well. "Let me tell you something," she said. "That man is no good. He beat their mother. Many times I had to doctor her myself. Always she refused to go to the hospital. He beat Cande, too." From her purse she pulled out a letter and handed it to the judge.

The judge called the attorneys to the stand. Each attorney read the letter silently before the judge summarized it to the people in court. "This letter declares that the house, which Ms. Torres' inherited before her marriage to Mr. Torres, be willed upon her death to Cande Torres. Ms. Torres felt that her husband was deliberately trying to beat her to death. She wanted Francisco to inherit the house, but he was in prison, so she willed it to Cande." The judge looked at each attorney, then at the jury. "Ms. Torres was not beaten to death, but her death was brought about by abuse and a stroke. This letter is to be considered as evidence that Mr. Torres abused and constantly assaulted his wife."

"Judge," Ms. Chavarría continued, "I promised Marta that I'd help Cande. He's such a good boy and is like his mother. He learned to take all the pain. As soon as that man's car would leave, I'd rush over to help Cande. *¡Ay, Dios mío!* That poor boy."

Beaver slumped forward and covered his face with his hands.

Ms. Rodríguez put her hand on his shoulder. "Do you need to go outside for a moment?"

Beaver was unable to speak and simply stayed where he was.

As the trial progressed, Beaver felt himself growing weaker; he felt as if his energy were being sucked out of his body. He also worried about Cande because he refused to speak. Cande was looking quite pale, and the dormitory mother said he was not eating. Being worried, both Beaver and Ms. Rodríguez took turns staying with him late into the night, each praying that the trial would be over quickly.

One day Beaver noticed that Ms. Rodríguez was restless and kept staring out the windows. "Relax, Ms. Rodríguez," Beaver suggested. "When this trial is over, you should take a cruise on a ship, or some kind of vacation."

"You don't do those things on a salary like mine, Beaver," she told him as she got up and went back to a chair near the window.

"I thought everyone who finished college got big salaries," Beaver stated.

Ms. Rodríguez laughed out loud. In fact, she laughed so hard that Beaver began to laugh loudly as well. They laughed together until talking was impossible. As Ms. Rodríguez dried her tears, the dorm mother appeared at the door, wondering what was going on. "It's okay, we were talking about college, that's all."

"That's great, but keep the noise down," the dorm mother said as she left the room.

Ms. Rodríguez looked at Beaver and said, "Thanks, I really needed to laugh. Sometimes, I think I've forgotten how to have fun."

"I know. It was like that for me in prison, but there was a guy who whistled a special tune. Sometimes late at night as I was trying to fall asleep, he'd whistle and I could hear the notes echo throughout the cell block. It was beautiful and so soothing. After his tune, I'd instantly fall asleep."

Ms. Rodríguez gazed at him silently. "You should have never been sent to prison," she said softly. "You're not the type."

Beaver shrugged. "It happened and I've got to deal with it now."

"Red Velvet Cake! I want you to bake a Red Velvet Cake for my birthday next week!" she suddenly exclaimed.

"No problem," said Beaver. "How old are you going to be?"

"Oh, Beaver, don't you know never to ask a girl her age?"

Beaver laughed. "I need to remember that."

The last day of the trial arrived. Beaver was nervous and Cande was fidgety. Ms. Rodríguez was constantly biting her lips and Ms. Turner looked very pale. They were all sitting on the same pew in the courtroom.

Mr. Torres was finally sentenced to thirty years in prison without parole. Beaver felt sorry for him.

He knew that the man would probably not survive the next two years in prison. Being off alcohol would more than likely kill him, and if it didn't, the other prisoners would probably finish him off. Child abusers were not liked by other prisoners. That much Beaver knew. For one split second, much to Beaver's horror, the old man turned and looked sternly into his son's eyes. In those dark eyes, Beaver saw not love, but only hatred. Immediately, Beaver looked at Cande, who was sketching on a note pad. He protectively put his arm around Cande's shoulders. "It's finally over, little brother," he whispered.

CHAPTER FOURTEEN

Beaver arrived at Hope State for his regular Sunday afternoon visit and found Cande in the activity room. He invited him for a walk. As Cande and Beaver moved slowly along the path that led from the church to the dormitory, Beaver listened as his younger brother talked.

"I love the craft classes," Cande stated happily, "especially painting. Eric and I are real friends. He helps me get around. We've adopted each other." Cande laughed.

"Hey, that's great! Eric's a good kid," Beaver said. "I've got some good news, too. I got a letter from Regina. She's now attending the University of Texas in Austin. She's real smart and her studies have paid off. She's going to study in England this summer."

"Wow!" Cande yelled. "Someday, I'll study in Paris, France!"

Beaver laughed. "And I'll attend the best cooking school in Paris!" They walked on a little further. "Do you want to see Texas play Oklahoma at the Cotton Bowl on New Year's Day?"

"That'd be great, Beaver."

"Jack has the tickets and he's invited us. I've always wanted to attend that game. The tickets are my birthday present from Jack!"

Cande laughed. "You know, I've adopted Jack as my grandfather. Maybe we can get Ms. Chavarría to fix Christmas dinner for the three of us. I'd like to get them together."

"You're asking for too much!" Beaver laughed.

Cande's cast had been removed in late September, but he felt no sensation in his leg, particularly from his hip to his knee. "It's like I'm walking on a wooden stump. There's no feeling," Cande complained. "I've still got to use these darn crutches."

"Give it time, Cande," Beaver said. "Your leg was crushed. The doctor said it'd be a good year or more before you felt better. Don't be in a hurry. There's plenty of time for you to get well and for you to paint."

"Oh, guess what! I meant to tell you right away. I've been accepted into the Arts Magnet High School. There, I'll be specializing in art!"

Beaver hugged him. "That's fantastic! I'm so happy for you." After a moment, Beaver added, "I told you everything was going to be fine."

Nonetheless, Beaver worried because Cande had not mentioned coming home in many months. He realized that Hope State offered Cande a safe haven, security, three meals a day, transportation here and there, and medical care. All Beaver could offer his brother was his love, but he never failed to mention that Cande could come home as soon as he could obtain his guardianship.

It was the first week in December when Beaver popped into Ms. Rodríguez's office for his monthly check-in.

She was standing in front of her file cabinet when he entered. "Beaver, come on in!" she said happily.

"Hi, Ms. Rodríguez. I see you're busy."

She smiled. "Yes, sometimes too busy, I think. How's school?"

"It's great! I've completed two semesters. Sometimes, I'm a little tired during the night classes, but it gets easier. Jack sold me his truck. He bought himself a new one, claiming that he needed one. I think he figured that I'd get home from school earlier at night if I didn't have to ride the bus." Beaver sat comfortably in the chair facing her desk.

"That's wonderful, Beaver. Give Jack my regards. I haven't seen him in months."

"He asks about you, too, Ms. Rodríguez. If you're in West Dallas, stop for a quick visit. He said to tell you that if your car needs repair to bring it to him and he'll work on it for no fee."

"I'll do that, Beaver," she said. "Don't forget that in January we go to court for your first attempt at guardianship."

"I know."

"The attorney said that it'll be tough, but we've got a fair chance as long as you've got a steady job with Jack. Your conduct has been impeccable and you can provide Cande with a home. All these things are in our favor. Besides, there's no one else to claim guardianship."

Beaver changed his position in the chair. "I have this feeling that Cande won't want to come home. I mean, he's got everything he needs at Hope State."

Ms. Rodríguez put down the papers she was holding. "You're his family and that's important to any child at Hope State. Remember that, Beaver. You're not out of his life by a long shot. Cande adores you."

She smiled at Beaver, then continued, "Are you going to visit him this Sunday afternoon?"

"Yes, I am," he said.

"I've got an idea. Why don't we meet at the dorm and bake brownies for all the kids. You can teach them how to make cookies and I'll bring the pizza."

"They'd like that!" Beaver answered.

"How is Ms. Chavarría? Maybe you can bring her over Sunday."

Beaver smiled. "She's fine. She drops by each evening just to chat. I'll invite her." He rose to leave.

"Oh, Beaver," Ms. Rodríguez said, "Don't worry, Cande will come home to you."

He smiled at her and nodded. As he left the office he realized that she was emerging as a friend. "Thanks, Ms. Rodríguez," Beaver muttered as he walked out into the street. "And, thank you, my

Lady," he whispered, "for sending me Joe Columbus, Jack and Ms. Rodríguez. I promise that when Cande comes home, we're going to take a trip down to Mexico to see your church and the cloak Juan Diego wore. Who knows, I might even take Joe Columbus and Jack. As for myself, I promise you that I'll help other people to repay the favors that Joe, Jack, and Ms. Rodríguez did for me. And, don't worry about me anymore, my Lady. I've got my life together."